Judy Christenberry

Triplet Secret Babies

HARLEQUIN®

TORONTO • NEW YORK • LONDON
AMSTERDAM • PARIS • SYDNEY • HAMBURG
STOCKHOLM • ATHENS • TOKYO • MILAN • MADRID
PRAGUE • WARSAW • BUDAPEST • AUCKLAND

Special thanks and acknowledgment are given to Judy Christenberry for her contribution to the MAITLAND MATERNITY: TRIPLETS, QUADS & QUINTS series.

ISBN 0-373-16901-9

TRIPLET SECRET BABIES

MAITLAND MATERNITY:
TRIPLETS, QUADS & QUINTS

You're invited to come back
to Maitland Maternity Hospital
to celebrate the opening of the
new McCallum Multiple Birth Wing, where
romances are born, secrets are revealed and
multiple bundles of joy are delivered!

Don't miss any of these heartwarming love stories!

TRIPLET SECRET BABIES
by Judy Christenberry
December 2001

QUADRUPLETS ON THE DOORSTEP
by Tina Leonard
January 2002

THE McCALLUM QUINTUPLETS
(3 stories in 1 volume)
featuring *New York Times* bestselling author
Kasey Michaels
Mindy Neff
Mary Anne Wilson
February 2002

Dear Reader,

Happy Holidays! Everyone at Harlequin American Romance wishes you joy and cheer at this wonderful time of year.

This month, bestselling author Judy Christenberry inaugurates MAITLAND MATERNITY: TRIPLETS, QUADS & QUINTS, our newest in-line continuity, with *Triplet Secret Babies*. In this exciting series, multiple births lead to remarkable love stories when Maitland Maternity Hospital opens a multiple birth wing. Look for *Quadruplets on the Doorstep* by Tina Leonard next month and *The McCallum Quintuplets* (3 stories in 1 volume) featuring *New York Times* bestselling author Kasey Michaels, Mindy Neff and Mary Anne Wilson in February.

In *The Doctor's Instant Family*, the latest book in Mindy Neff's BACHELORS OF SHOTGUN RIDGE miniseries, a sexy and single M.D. is intrigued by his mysterious new office assistant. Can the small-town doctor convince the single mom to trust him with her secrets—and her heart? Next, temperatures rise when a handsome modern-day swashbuckler offers to be nanny to three little girls in exchange for access to a plain-Jane professor's house in *Her Passionate Pirate* by Neesa Hart. And let us welcome a new author to the Harlequin American Romance family. Kathleen Webb makes her sparkling debut with *Cindrella's Shoe Size*.

Enjoy this month's offerings, and make sure to return each and every month to Harlequin American Romance!

Wishing you happy reading,

Melissa Jeglinski
Associate Senior Editor
Harlequin American Romance

ABOUT THE AUTHOR

Judy Christenberry has been writing romances for fifteen years because she loves happy endings as much as her readers do. A former French teacher, Judy now devotes herself to writing full-time. She hopes readers have as much fun reading her stories as she does writing them. She spends her spare time reading, watching her favorite sports teams and keeping track of her two daughters. Judy's a native Texan, but now lives in Arizona.

Books by Judy Christenberry

HARLEQUIN AMERICAN ROMANCE

*Brides for Brothers
†Tots for Texans

Don't miss any of our special offers. Write to us at the following address for information on our newest releases.

Harlequin Reader Service
U.S.: 3010 Walden Ave., P.O. Box 1325, Buffalo, NY 14269
Canadian: P.O. Box 609, Fort Erie, Ont. L2A 5X3

CAST OF CHARACTERS

Jackson McCallum—Patriarch of the McCallum family. He dedicated the new multiple-birth wing to Maitland Maternity Hospital to honor the memory of his late wife.

Briana McCallum—Jackson's middle triplet. She's pregnant with triplets of her own, but won't reveal the identity of the daddy-to-be.

Hunter Callaghan—Director of McCallum Multiple Birth Wing. His arrival at Maitland Maternity has raised a few eyebrows, especially since there is no denying the red-hot sparks between him and a certain expectant mother.

Adam and Maggie McCallum—Jackson's eldest triplet son and his daughter-in-law. They want to start a family of their own and hope the specialists at Maitland Maternity can help make their dream come true.

Caleb McCallum—Jackson's youngest triplet. The ex-police officer doesn't want to settle down, but he might find love where he least expects it. Read about his story in *Quadruplets on the Doorstep* coming next month.

Chapter One

Her head was beating like a bass drum during a pep rally. Briana McCallum stared at the shelf of pain relievers in the New York deli she'd found a block from the hotel, feeling lucky to have found it open after midnight.

There it was! Her favorite relief for headaches. She grabbed it and then took a soda from the refrigerated shelf nearby and hurried to the cash register.

She was digging through her purse when the clerk said, "You give me your money."

"Yes, I'm looking for it," she assured him, her head down as she dug through her bag for her billfold.

"No, all your money," he returned harshly.

She looked up to find herself staring down the barrel of a pistol pointed directly at her.

"What—" she began, confused, when the outer door opened and another customer arrived. Relief poured through her. She wasn't alone with the wacko anymore. The pistol swung away from her to the new arrival.

"You come. Give me money," the clerk ordered.

The new arrival, a handsome man in a tuxedo, his tie untied, stared in surprise. "What's going on?"

He looked at Briana for an explanation. "I think he's planning on robbing us," she said.

"I go home now. I need money," the clerk said, as if that explained everything.

"Home to—?" the man asked.

"India. My mother sick. I go home. Give me money."

After a dead silence, the man behind the counter began shifting, swinging the gun between the two of them, and Briana grew more nervous. "I—I don't have a lot of money." She pulled out about sixty dollars and laid it on the counter. "That's all I have with me."

"Now you," the clerk said, scooping up the money and looking at the man.

With reluctance, the man pulled out his wallet from his back pants pocket. He took the cash out and laid it on the counter. Then he tucked his wallet away. "That's all I've got."

It was considerably more than Briana carried with her.

But she was distracted from thinking about that. The clerk came around the counter and gestured for them to go to the back of the store. Was he going to shoot them before he left? She didn't want to die, not when her dream was just coming true. Not when she'd finally achieved—

"Go!" the clerk shouted, becoming more agitated.

The man put his hands on her shoulders and pushed her gently in front of him, keeping himself between her and the gun. A very protective gesture. One her brother Caleb would approve of. As did she.

They reached the back of the store and the clerk shoved open a door that said Employees Only. It was dark, not a large area, and she was reluctant to go in. Suddenly the man fell into her and she fell to her knees on the concrete floor. She heard a loud slamming noise and everything went black.

She thought she'd passed out, but she was still awake. Then she realized the door behind them had been slammed shut and there was no light.

"Are you okay?" the deep voice of the other customer asked. His hands found her shoulders again and he half lifted her to her feet.

"Yes, just bruised," she said softly. "Are we—"

"Locked in." He turned her loose and took a step back. In the darkness she felt abandoned.

Then a bright light came on.

She stared around her before her gaze returned to her companion. He'd found the light switch by the door and turned it on. She was grateful. Nothing seemed quite so bad when there was light.

"Thank you. I'm glad we're not left in the dark."

"I guess. But the accommodations aren't too posh."

She couldn't argue with that assessment. They were in a small storeroom, the shelves packed with food items from floor to ceiling. The only piece of furniture was a sturdy stool, dingy white in color.

"At least we're alive," Briana pointed out. "I've heard of too many of these robberies where the witnesses were killed."

"Yeah. I guess since he's leaving the country, he doesn't think we can hurt him." The man prowled the storeroom, pacing from one end to the other. "I tried the door. I don't think I can force it open."

"Won't we be okay? I mean, someone will come in to relieve him after a while, won't they? If we just wait, he'll let us out."

The man looked at his watch. "Probably at seven, six if we're lucky. Which means we have about five and half hours in this hellhole."

She noticed his watch was a Rolex, which went well with his tux. Obviously not a man down on his luck. "Um, are you from New York?" she asked.

"No. Say, you don't happen to have a cell phone, do you?" He turned and stared at her, his blue-eyed gaze enough to convince Briana to tell him the truth and nothing but.

"Yes, but I didn't bring it with me. I didn't think I'd need it in New York City."

"Me, neither." He began pacing again. After a minute, he said, "Obviously you're not from New York, either."

"No, Texas."

"Ah. I'm from Chicago. The name's Hunter." He

stuck out a large hand with slim strong fingers, a hand almost artistic in appearance except for its size.

"Briana," she said. She tried to avoid using her last name with strangers, in case they knew of her family wealth. She'd been both pursued and rejected because of it.

"Unusual name."

"I'm part of ABC."

"I beg your pardon?" he asked, one eyebrow raised.

"I'm the second of triplets. My older brother is Adam, I'm Briana, and my younger brother is Caleb. ABC."

"Very clever."

"Not really. That's what they called us until Dad got around to naming us."

"I see," he said, but Briana knew he didn't. She'd left some information out of her explanation.

Then she thought she heard something. "Listen! Is that someone in the store?"

He came toward the door, nearer to her, and placed his ear against the wood. "I don't hear anything."

"I don't now, either. It was just a rustling sound. Or maybe it was my imagination," she admitted with a sigh. She put her fingers to her temples and massaged. Her headache was as bad as ever. Wait! The medicine she'd been about to buy. She'd stuck it and the soda in her handbag without thinking when the clerk had ordered them to the back of the store.

Her bag, large, one that could hold all kinds of

necessities, was on the floor. She grabbed it, moaning as she stood. The motion wasn't helping her headache.

"Are you all right?" Hunter asked.

"Yes, it's just my headache. That's why I was here. I didn't have any pain reliever in my room and the hotel clerk sent me here. I think I'll sue him." She smiled to let her companion know she was joking. Digging into her purse, she found the unopened medicine and the soda. "Aha!"

He stared at her. "You managed to get what you needed."

"Yes, I did," she agreed as she tore at the wrapping. "Assuming I can ever get it unwrapped."

"Here," he said, taking the package away from her and deftly ripping the box open. He removed the bottle and quickly lined up the arrows to pop the lid off. "How many do you want, one or two?"

"Three," she said distinctly, holding out her hand.

"Three? I don't think that's a good idea."

In spite of his helpfulness, she wasn't happy with his interference. "Look, unless you're a doctor—"

"I am."

That response stopped her in her tracks. She was attending a medical conference on multiple births and a number of doctors had been in attendance. That would be too much of a coincidence, wouldn't it?

"It doesn't matter. I take this medicine all the time. When a headache isn't stopped early, I need three tablets to make it go away."

Without another word, he tapped the bottle and put three tablets in her hand. She popped the lid of the soda and tossed the pills in her mouth, then swallowed some of the liquid.

"I guess I should save the rest of the soda. Did you want a drink?" she asked, remembering he was a victim, too.

He hesitated, then said, "Yeah, I'll take a sip, along with a couple of pills, if you don't mind sharing."

"Of course not. Is that why you're here, too?"

"Actually, I thought I'd get some milk to drink. My stomach needed settling."

"I don't think you're supposed to drink milk if you're queasy," she said.

"Unless you're a doctor..." he said, challenging her with his blue eyes.

Quickly, she disavowed that occupation. She'd wanted to be a doctor, but she discovered as a teenager that blood made her pass out. That rather eliminated medicine as a profession. She'd chosen the next best thing, a hospital administrator.

"Is there any milk in here?" she asked, looking around.

"No, this part has no refrigeration. There's some sodas, sports drinks, stuff like that. No milk. But I guess we won't starve to death."

"You mean we should help ourselves to their food? But wouldn't that be stealing?"

He shook his head, grinning. "Not unless you're a

purist. I think I already paid about a hundred and fifty dollars. That should cover a few Twinkies.''

''Twinkies? Do they have Twinkies?'' Normally, she restrained her junk-food urge. But stress, along with her headache, made her weak. Twinkies sounded perfect.

With a chuckle, the man reached up to a shelf behind her and drew down a box. He carefully examined the box before breaking it open.

''What were you looking for?'' she asked, puzzled.

''Just checking. Here, have one. They're individually wrapped.''

She took one and opened the cellophane, eager to taste the gooey sweetness. ''Um, thank you. I may survive after all.''

''Is the headache gone?''

''It's easing.''

''Well, you might as well be comfortable.'' He stepped away and reached for the stool, placing it in the center of the storeroom. ''Here's your chair.''

His generosity reminded her of how he'd shielded her from the gun. The man was a true gentleman. ''It wouldn't be fair for me to take the only seat.''

He looked surprised. ''You think I should sit while you stand? My mama didn't raise me that way.''

''No, but we could share,'' she assured him, smiling.

He looked even more surprised. ''It's not that big a stool.''

Realizing he thought she meant they could both

occupy the stool at once, she turned bright red. "No! No, I meant we could take turns."

A lopsided grin that only increased his sexiness was his initial response. "Darn, I was having some great images in my head."

She didn't want to think about those images. In fact, she thought the more distance she kept from this man, the better off she'd be. He was too handsome for his own good. "I'll take a turn first," she said and sat down on the stool, taking another bite of her Twinkie.

"Good decision," he said and started pacing again.

"Maybe if you leaned against the shelves, it would be easier for you," she suggested, her gaze following him as he moved. He was a big man. She wasn't short, five-seven, but he had to be over six feet tall. Though there were a few grey hairs at his temples, they blended in with his blond hair, cut short. Very businesslike.

"No, thanks," he said and continued to pace.

A big, hardheaded man. Fine, let him wear himself out pacing. She didn't care!

She finished her Twinkie, and he offered another.

"No. You didn't eat one."

"Not yet. I'm sure I will before the evening's over. My dinner was good. I had steak."

Again Briana thought of her conference. They'd served steak at the banquet tonight. "What conference were you attending?"

"It was a conference about multiple births. I specialize in obstetrics, particularly at-risk pregnancies."

"Oh." The same conference. It was a wonder she hadn't met him already. But she'd been interested in the administrative side of multiple births. Not the medical procedures being discussed.

"Not interested, even though you're a multiple? Especially when any pregnancy you might have could be multiple?"

"No."

"Have you had a pregnancy already?"

"No, I haven't. Have you?"

"I assume you mean as a father, not as a mother."

She rolled her eyes. The man thought he had a sense of humor. Ha!

"No. Me, neither. I hope to, someday."

"I don't want to be rude, but aren't you getting a little old for a first-time dad?"

"I'm under forty, by two years. Men aren't as affected by the biological clock as women. How about you? Is your clock ticking?"

"I'm thirty-one if that's what you're asking," she said, irritation in her voice. She'd thought a lot about having a baby, but she'd promised herself, no baby until she found a father, one she could love and trust. She'd been betrayed once, and she was determined that wasn't going to happen again.

He must've realized he'd upset her. With a soothing voice, he said, "You still have plenty of time."

She ducked her head. She'd been rude, and he was

trying to comfort her. "I'm sorry. That conversation was my fault, and I was rude."

"Don't worry about it. Have another Twinkie. It will sweeten you up." He presented it to her with a flourish.

She took his offering. She didn't want to be rude again. Slowly she unwrapped it and took a bite.

At the same time, he said, "What kind of conference were you attending?"

She choked. She should've been prepared, but his charm had distracted her. He came to her side and pounded on her back.

"Are you all right?" he asked.

"Fine. Please, that's enough," she added as he continued to slap her back.

"Sorry. Choking is dangerous. Maybe I should've tried the Heimlich maneuver."

"No, it just went down the wrong way. I'm fine now," she added. She hoped he'd move away from her. His distinctive male scent was enticing.

"Okay. What conference are you attending?"

She finally mumbled, "The same one."

He frowned and took a step closer instead of backing off. "What did you say?"

"I'm attending the same conference," she admitted, speaking clearly.

"You're a medical professional?"

"Not exactly."

"What do you mean by not exactly?" he demanded, his hands on his hips.

"I'm in medical administration."

"Oh. I guess that explains why I didn't meet you. The joint sessions were pretty big."

"Yes."

HUNTER CALLAGHAN stared at the beauty sitting on the old stool. She was dressed in jeans and a sweater, her light brown hair framing her delicate features and curving under as it reached her shoulders. It was the hazel eyes, however, that drew him the most.

"Suddenly you don't want to talk?" he asked, distracted by her strange attitude.

She shrugged but said nothing.

"Did you enjoy the conference?"

She shrugged again. Then she added, "Look, I came to learn all I could. I'm not very experienced."

"There's nothing wrong with that," he said, crossing his arms over his chest as he stared at her. Something was going on here, and he wanted to know what it was.

"I'm tired," she muttered, in an obvious attempt to change the subject.

"No wonder, it's almost two o'clock in the morning."

She slid down from the stool. "I think it's your turn to sit down. We should probably change every half hour."

"I don't need to sit. You go ahead."

"No, I insist. I appreciate your gentlemanly behavior, but I don't want to take advantage." Standing, she came to his shoulder. Good. He hated short women who made him feel awkward. Not that it mattered. In a few hours he wouldn't see her again.

Since she insisted, he took a seat on the stool, hooking the heels of his dress shoes over the lower rung. "Uh, Briana," he said, trying to figure out if he was going to freak her out with what he had to say. But he had to warn her.

"Yes?"

"If you walk around, stay away from that back corner," he said as casually as he could. He was hoping she wouldn't ask why.

But of course she did.

"Why?"

"Well, I think that's a rat trap. And I wouldn't want you to get caught in it. I'm not sure I could free you."

She paled and took a step closer to him, unusual on her part. He'd noticed she was more comfortable if he didn't come close.

"A—a rat trap?" she asked, her voice trembling.

"Yeah."

"That's why you examined the Twinkie box? But it's on a high shelf. Surely a rat couldn't get to it way up there?"

"It's my understanding they can climb well."

She took another step closer to him. "That's why you wouldn't lean against the shelves?" Horror had her shaking all over.

''Briana, they're not going to attack us. I just wanted you to be careful.''

His words didn't calm her. She pressed against his side, her gaze swerving around the room. ''Have you seen any?''

''No. Probably the trap has been efficient and we won't see any at all. I'm probably being an alarmist.'' In spite of the noises he'd heard. She'd heard them, too, when they'd first entered the room, and thought someone was in the store. He looped his arm around her, liking the feel of her, the smell of her.

Great. That's all he needed, to become uncomfortably aroused in addition to everything else. He was a little surprised by his response. The last few years, he'd found himself less and less attracted to the women who pursued doctors.

She broke from his hold. ''I'm sorry. I'm being silly. There probably aren't any rats in here, right? I'll just stay away from that corner,'' she promised, her lips trembling as she stepped away from him.

For several minutes she paced around the room and he had the pleasure of watching her. Her figure was worth looking at, especially in the snug-fitting jeans. He finally closed his eyes, trying to distract his mind with thoughts of operating procedures.

But those kinds of methodical thoughts had no chance over a beautiful woman in jeans. With a sigh, he opened his eyes, trying to think of a conversational topic that would distract both of them.

Instead, the silence was broken by a terrible clang. Something had been caught in the trap.

He looked at Briana, knowing it wasn't her but wanting to make sure she was all right. He saw her just in time to catch her as she rushed to him and climbed the step stool as if it was a ladder.

She ended up in his lap, her legs wrapped around him, her arms tightening around his neck.

"Wow, why didn't I think of sharing?" he said, a smile on his lips.

Chapter Two

Hunter sat holding a warm, trembling female, unsure what to do next. He didn't mind holding her. In fact, sitting as they were, things were getting interesting. But she might object, since she'd already been leery of him.

"I know I should get down," she muttered against his neck, sending tingling sensations through his body, "but I can't."

"Why not?"

"I have a phobia about rats."

"A phobia?"

"Yes, an unreasonable fear of something."

He chuckled. "I'm a doctor, remember? I know what a phobia is."

"Well, mine is rats. I was okay as long as I could convince myself they wouldn't really show up here, but—but is it a rat in the trap?"

"Looks like it to me," he said, staring over her shoulder. "I can't be sure until I go over there."

She squeezed him tighter. "No! No, don't go over there! He might bite you."

"How did you get a phobia about rats?" He cuddled her a little closer, liking the feel of her, her scent. "Were you raised in a slum?"

"No, not at all! We had a very nice house, but I saw a movie about a little boy and the rats—terrorized him. I screamed every night for weeks. My brothers laughed at me. Finally my father let me keep a cat in my room all night so I'd be protected."

Her voice trembled, and Hunter had an immediate picture of that little girl, wildly afraid of rats, pleading for protection. He held her more tightly against him. "It's all right. You're safe, Briana. I won't let the rats get you."

"Are you laughing at me?" she asked, her voice small.

"No. I'm not laughing. I'm understanding."

"Oh. Thank you. But we can't—I mean, we can't—this isn't seemly."

Ah. He knew what was causing her concern. "Look, Bri," he said, shortening her name, "men react to stimuli without any, uh, intent. It's not something they can control. I promise I won't take advantage."

"But it must be uncomfortable."

"If I were wearing jeans, it would be. They don't allow much wiggle room, uh, I mean, extra space." He was discovering any extra space he had was disappearing rapidly. He said, "Maybe I should go over and look. Maybe it's just a really big mouse. Would that be better?''

''I don't think you should go over there,'' she said, the trembling starting again.

''I won't get close, I promise,'' he said gently and placed his hands on her arms, deadlocked around his neck.

''Come on, Bri, turn loose. I'll come right back, I promise.''

''And I can stay on the stool?''

''Of course. You can even have another Twinkie.''

''No. Treats never help. Dad tried that.''

''I bet he did,'' Hunter muttered. Slowly he got her to lower her arms. Putting his hands on her waist, he slipped off the stool and swung her on top of it.

As he turned away, she reached out for him. ''Hunter, be careful.''

''I will, Bri, I promise.''

He walked over to the corner and stared at the dead animal. It was definitely a rat, a large one. Could he get away with telling Bri it was a big mouse? He was afraid she'd realize he was lying. He'd never been good at lying.

He came back to the stool.

She held out her arms, as if ready to resume her position in his lap. He shook his head. ''I'm going to walk around for a while, to stretch my legs.''

''And what was it?''

He hung his head. He hated to tell her. ''It was a rat. But it's definitely dead.''

She reached for him, her hold probably leaving bruises on his skin. "You'd better get back up here with me. We'll be safe here."

He wasn't going to discuss the safety of the stool. If he took that refuge away from her, she'd go to pieces. "Nope, I'll be safe enough out here in the open."

He began to pace, but thought of a question he'd wanted to ask. "You know, when you've talked about your childhood, you never mention your mother. Where was she?"

"She died when we were born."

"Why?"

"She bled to death. That's why Dad—uh, it was sad for my father, but we didn't know the difference."

"Didn't he ever remarry?"

She shook her head, but she kept her gaze fastened to the trap in the corner.

"But your dad took care of the three of you?" Somehow, he wanted to know she'd been okay.

She shrugged. "He hired someone."

Hunter was surprised by the anger mixed with sorrow he felt. "He hired someone? He didn't take care of you himself?"

"He was busy. And he doesn't seem to care for babies. Once we got old enough to talk, to understand, he began to take a little interest in us."

"Hence the cat?"

Briana shot him a rueful smile. "That was the first

time he listened to me. And then only because I was disrupting his peace. But I believed it was because he loved me. More than my brothers. It satisfied me for several years. I'd tell myself the cat was there because he loved me, even if he couldn't spend time with me.''

''How did your brothers react?''

''They hated the cat. And teased it a couple of times when they caught it. But then it scratched them and they backed off.''

He'd taken a lot of psychology classes and was fascinated with children's coping mechanisms. ''And when did you demand more attention?''

''How do you know I did?'' She wouldn't look at him and he grinned, stepped closer and slid his arms around her waist. He liked holding her close.

''Just a hunch,'' he said with a grin. Her memories seemed to relax her, and that was a good thing.

''Actually, my brothers took action first. They became little hellions. Again, my father's peace was cut up. He demanded Grace make them behave. Grace and her husband, Douglas, took care of us. Grace looked him in the eye and told him if he didn't participate in his children's lives, there wasn't anything she could do.''

''Wise woman.''

''Yes, and brave. Dad wasn't an easy man to face down. He'd been grieving about our mother's death and paying attention to business. It was easier to leave us to someone else. But to his credit, that's when he changed. We'd started school, and he'd discovered we had minds.''

Hunter lifted one hand and cupped her soft, warm cheek. "So then your father loved you?"

She shrugged again. "That's when he played a part in our lives. By the time we graduated from college, I think he loved us. We've been a family the last few years.''

He pulled her against him and rubbed her back.

"What about you? Did you have the perfect childhood?"

"I suppose I did. My dad was a doctor, had a small practice in the country, handled all kinds of emergencies. My mom was always there for me and my brother. Not that we realized we had anything special. Now I do.''

She pushed away from him. "And I suppose that's the kind of woman you'll marry for your future kids. So they'll have the same life."

There was a bitterness in her voice that made him raise his eyebrows. "Wouldn't everyone want the same thing? Wouldn't you have preferred to have a mother?"

"Of course I would!" she snapped.

"Whoa, there, lady. What did I say wrong?"

"Nothing. What time is it?"

"Almost three. Are you exhausted?" He'd give her her change of subject. Things were stressful enough for her as it was.

"Yes. I didn't get much sleep during the conference. I didn't want to miss anything,'' she said, rubbing one temple.

"Did your headache ever go away?'' he asked, taking her pulse at her neck.

"Yes, mostly.''

"Look, why don't you—I can hold you and let you sleep a little. That's probably the only thing that will give you any relief, and it will make the time pass faster. Before you know it, it will be morning and your nightmare will be over.''

"That's not fair to you,'' she said doubtfully, staring at him. "And it's—you know what happened last time.''

"I explained it's something a man can't control. But nothing happened, remember?'' He was glad she couldn't read his mind. Holding her again was becoming an obsession for him.

Finally, she slid off the stool, standing next to it. "If you're sure you don't mind. I'd give a lot to get a few minutes of sleep.''

"I don't mind.'' He climbed onto the stool and held out his arms. Slowly, unlike the last time, she responded to his invitation. She settled in his lap, but she seemed unsure where to put her hands.

"Wrap your arms around me,'' he suggested, "and lay your head on my chest.''

She did so, and he held her in place, feeling a surprising peace settle in him. He had her safe in his arms. Softly rubbing her back, he whispered, "You're safe now. Just relax.''

After several minutes, her body began to relax and grow heavy against him. She was asleep.

AS BRIANA settled into Hunter's embrace, she knew she was being weak. But she'd reached her limit, and she didn't mind admitting it.

And she'd never met such a strong man, physically and mentally. He'd been calm and protective. It seemed all her life she'd been competing with her brothers. She loved them dearly, but being one of triplets, and the only female, made life difficult.

So, just once in her life, she was going to accept her weakness and give in to the protection this man offered. Besides, it felt so good to be in his arms. As she laid her head against his chest, his heart beat a steady rhythm that lulled her in to relaxation, and she closed her eyes.

SATISFACTION filled Hunter as he realized Briana was getting the rest she so desperately needed. Apparently she'd been a lot more intense about the conference than him. He'd attended a few before. Besides, as a doctor, he'd pulled a few long nights as he came through medical school.

He checked his watch. They only had a couple more hours if the morning guy came in at six o'clock. His arms tightened around Briana as she rested against him. He'd love to be able to return to his comfortable bed in the hotel, but he wouldn't want to turn Briana loose anyway.

That thought brought him up short. What was he thinking? They'd part as soon as morning came, of course. She was from Texas. He was from Chicago. Maybe they'd see each other at future conventions and laugh about their adventure in a New York deli.

He thought again of Briana as a little girl, frightened by a movie. She'd sounded so alone as she'd told him about her phobia. She must've been adorable as a child. How could her father have ignored her?

Of course, he'd eventually responded to her fears and allowed her to keep a cat in her room. He supposed that showed the man's humanity.

But he'd want more than humanity for his children. He intended to love them and be there for them. He looked down at the brunette beauty in his arms. They'd make beautiful babies together, he decided. "Should that ever come up in the future," he quickly amended with a rumble of laughter.

She stirred in his arms, her eyes fluttering open. "Everything okay?" she muttered.

He kissed her forehead and drew her closer. "Everything's fine. You're safe. Go back to sleep," he whispered. Almost before he finished speaking, she dropped off to sleep again.

His body was responding, as it had earlier, to her closeness, but it was to be expected. He shifted a little, hoping his movement wouldn't awaken her.

He wished they'd talked longer. He'd like to know about her situation, what job she held, her personal life. Hell, he didn't even know if she had a boyfriend.

She must. She was too pretty, too dynamic, to be alone. Unless all the men in Texas were dummies, and that's not what he'd heard.

He didn't like the idea that someone else would hold her. A ridiculous thought, but he felt possessive about her. He'd saved her from the rats. She was his to protect.

He decided that kind of thinking was dangerous, so he tried to concentrate on a new theory introduced at the conference about treating at-risk pregnancies. Anything to take his mind off the woman in his arms.

AN HOUR LATER, Hunter eased off the stool. He had to stand before his rear became permanently attached to the hard surface of the stool. His arms slid beneath Briana's bottom. He was glad he worked out regularly, or he wouldn't be able to stand and hold her, too. Slowly, he maneuvered his way around the storeroom. Still another hour or two before the morning guy would arrive. He looked at the stool, not sure he could sit again.

But he wasn't sure either that he could stand with Briana in his arms until someone came. And he didn't want to wake her up.

"My choices are limited," he muttered. Finally, he pushed the stool toward the thick door. When he got the stool directly in front of the door, he shoved it a little to one side. Then he settled back onto the stool, managing to arrange Briana's sleeping form in a more comfortable position.

He'd have to give her credit. When she slept, she really slept. She hadn't shown any signs of waking up the entire time he moved around.

After she was settled, he slowly leaned his back against the door and felt relief at the support. Then he let his head rest there, too. Could he sleep at all and maintain his balance? He was kind of wedged up between the door and the edge of the shelving.

He'd just doze.

It would be all right.

SOMETHING was bothering her.

Briana shook her head, irritated by the noise that was disrupting her sleep. Then it stopped. She settled back against the mattress, the comforting throb soothing her again. This was a great bed, she decided. It held her close.

Even at the thought, arms tightened around her.

Arms? Mattresses don't have arms, do they? Briana wasn't ready to wake up, but that strange question forced her to open her eyes.

The first thing she realized was that she was upright, leaning against—a man. Suddenly she remembered where she was and what had happened. Hunter. She was leaning against Hunter.

He'd fallen asleep leaning against the door. She checked her watch. It was five after seven. "Hunter?" she whispered.

He hugged her against him, as if he thought she

was asking him to keep her safe. It did feel good, but that wasn't the point.

"Hunter, there should be someone here now," she whispered. "Shouldn't we shout or something?"

He sat upright suddenly, shifting Briana. "What?"

"It's after seven."

"After seven? Haven't you heard anyone outside?"

"I don't know. Something woke me."

He stood abruptly, and Briana found herself held in his arms.

"You—you can put me down," she insisted.

He let her slide down his body, an interesting trip to say the least, and suddenly she was standing on her feet.

"Can you stand?" he asked, still holding on to her.

"Of course. Can you, after I've used you for a bed all night?"

He smiled, but Briana noticed the strain around his eyes and the weariness. "I think so. I'm just a little stiff." He moved the stool away from the door and beat on it as he yelled.

They both heard a startled exclamation. Hunter grinned at Briana like a caveman who had found meat for his family.

"Who's in there?"

Whoever asked that question sounded more afraid of them than she was of the rats. "We're customers who got locked in last night. Please let us out."

"Oh! Yes. Yes, I will!"

When the door opened, they discovered an elderly

woman wearing an apron, a look of horror on her face. ''Who locked you in?'' she wanted to know.

Hunter took over. ''The clerk who was working last night. He robbed us of what cash we had and put us in here before he left. He also cleaned out your cash register.''

''So, it wasn't a thief?''

''No, it wasn't. Now, if you'll excuse us, we'd like to get back to our hotel,'' he said, gently moving the woman to one side. Then he reached out for Briana's hand.

She gladly gave him her hand. It made her feel under his protection, as she'd been all night. He pulled her toward the door.

''Aren't we going to stay and talk to the police?'' she asked him in a low voice.

''Do you believe it will help them catch the guy?'' he asked.

''No, of course not.''

''Then what's the point? If we stay, we won't catch our planes, and I have to be back in Chicago for a special surgery in the morning.''

He had a point. ''Okay, we'll leave our names and addresses and they can contact us if they need to.'' They each wrote their information down and gave it to the owner.

They emerged into a busy world. There were car fumes, noisy taxis, people everywhere, which seemed strange after there having only been the two of them for the past few hours.

It was half a block to the conference hotel. When they reached the entrance, he wrapped his arm around her shoulders. ''They're going to think we've been out partying all night,'' he muttered. ''Hope we don't see anyone from the conference or the rumors will fly.''

She hadn't thought of that. She certainly didn't want rumors of her pulling an all-nighter with a handsome doctor. She was working too hard to prove herself. She ducked her head and both of them walked fast.

They managed to snag an elevator at once and when the doors closed, leaving them alone, they both breathed a sigh of relief.

''Glad to be alone again?'' he asked with a weary smile.

''Surprisingly, yes. This would've been awkward to explain.''

''Awkward? It would've been impossible. Is there a husband around who is going to read you the riot act?''

It was a little late to be asking that question, but Hunter had been a perfect gentleman from the beginning. She shook her head. ''No husband.''

He looped his arms around her, pulling her closer to rest against his body. ''I'm glad.''

''Any wife?''

''Nope, not even a girlfriend.''

He put a finger under her chin, and, before she realized what was going on, he kissed her.

Chapter Three

There were people waiting when the elevator door opened on her floor. Briana, who'd been enjoying the kiss as much as Hunter seemed to be, was grateful she didn't know any of them.

"Uh, out, please." She kept her eyes lowered. She didn't want anyone, even strangers, to see the effect of Hunter's kiss. Her lips still tingled and she felt a surprising desire to repeat their behavior.

Hunter followed her off the elevator.

"Your room is on this floor, too?" she asked in surprise and uneasiness. She needed distance to avoid doing something unwise.

"No, I'm escorting you to your room," he assured her.

Always a gentleman.

"Look, Hunter, I know you must be exhausted. I certainly am. Don't worry about me. I'll be fine."

'It's kind of become a habit," he said with a charming smile, "worrying about you."

She dug her plastic key card out of her jeans pocket

where she'd put it only a few hours ago, though it seemed like a lifetime. "This is my room," she assured him as she stopped in front of a door and inserted the key card. The small light turned from red to green and she shoved the door open.

Hunter followed her in so that when she turned to thank him for his...whatever, he was there. And his arms were around her again. And he looked as if he was about to repeat the embrace they'd shared on the elevator.

It had been an incredible kiss, one she'd felt to her very toes. Unlike any she'd ever had before. But that was probably because they'd spent so much time together, really together.

She should stop him. But curiosity, wondering if it had really been that good a kiss, welcomed him. Her arms went around his neck, her body pressed against his. Her lips, when he touched them with his, leapt to mate with him.

Three or four kisses later, Hunter, breathing heavily, managed to say "Briana."

She thought it was a good thing he could remember her name, because his kisses had scrambled her brain. All she could think about was him...and getting closer. It wasn't like her to respond so completely to a man's touch. But Hunter's touch had a magical effect on her. "Hunter," she murmured in response.

"Sweetheart," he muttered, "I need you."

Instead of bothering with words, she pulled him toward the bed. They fell on it with a sigh of relief and resumed kissing. He was the most incredible kisser.

Tuxedo studs went flying as Briana's fingers went to work. It occurred to her that later she might regret such abandon, but it felt wonderful now. As more and more of his muscular chest, with blond hairs winding their way down it, came into view, the happier she became.

Each of them removed clothing piece by piece, exposing the other. But Briana never felt awkward or uncomfortable. She was too involved in what was going on. It seemed right that, after their night of togetherness, they should be completely together.

As a lover, Hunter was as gentlemanly and considerate as he'd been all night. But there was an edge of need that made her heart beat faster. He stroked and urged her closer, his mouth consuming hers. When he entered her, she felt completely loved and cradled, protected, until an urgency began that drove her even closer.

Then there was no conscious thought, just emotions, feelings, a consuming fire that left her exhausted yet sated. Hunter fell against her as he, too, reached the zenith of feelings. She held him close.

As she sank into a drifting state of sensations, he pushed up from the bed. "Did I hurt you, Bri? Are you all right?"

"I'm wonderful, Hunter, absolutely…wonderful." She never opened her eyes. And that was the last she remembered.

HUNTER STARED DOWN at the beautiful face. It seemed most of the time he'd had with her, her eyes had been closed. But he remembered their hazel beauty. He remembered everything about her.

He'd never experienced such emotions, such sensations in making love before. It had never been so overpowering. Briana was clearly a special woman, but there'd been so little time. He truly hadn't intended to make love to her when he'd followed her into the room. All he'd wanted was one more kiss. The kiss in the elevator had been so special, so…he couldn't come up with another word to describe it.

His hand cupped her soft cheek as she slept. He didn't want to leave her, but he needed a shower and clean clothes. If he changed now, while she slept, he'd be back before she even knew he was gone. Then he'd take her to breakfast.

They had a lot to discuss. He had no intention of letting her walk away with no plans for the future. She was his to protect, to love, to cherish. That much he knew. He thought she knew it, too.

They'd plan a future. They'd compromise. Somehow they'd find a way to be together. Because Briana…he suddenly realized he didn't even know her last name. But he'd take care of that detail. Finally he'd found the one woman in the world who made his life complete. They'd find a way to be together.

After rubbing his lips over hers, he slid from the bed and searched for his clothing. He found everything but one of the studs for the tuxedo shirt. He smiled as he remembered Briana dispensing with them recklessly. He'd loved that about her. She was an enthusiastic lover, making him feel wanted, a great aphrodisiac.

Longingly, he stared once more at her sprawled under the sheet with which he'd covered her. As tired as he was, he wanted to make love to her all over again. And he suspected he'd feel that way the rest of his life.

He whispered, "I'll be back soon, sweetheart." Then he left her hotel room to climb the flight of stairs at the end of the corridor. He was on the next floor. Not far away. He hurried, unable to stand being away from her any longer than he had to.

THE BUZZING of an alarm awakened Briana from a deep sleep. She flailed at the noise and found the snooze button, she supposed, because the noise stopped. She drifted back to sleep.

Five minutes later, the noise repeated itself. This time she opened her eyes, barely, and noted the time. Eight-o-five. She sat up in bed. Her flight left La-Guardia Airport at nine-forty-five. She needed to catch a taxi by eight-thirty. She'd set the alarm last night before she ventured out of the hotel. She leapt from the bed and suddenly realized she was naked. A flood of memories held her frozen as the events of the night and, in particular, the morning hit her.

She'd made love to Hunter!

She looked around the room as if expecting him to

pop out from behind the dresser. He'd left? Disappeared? Or had she dreamed the entire thing?

She really didn't know. She was still exhausted and wasn't thinking too clearly. She moved toward the bathroom, sure a shower would help, when she winced in pain and hopped on her left foot. Bending down, she discovered a stud for a tuxedo shirt in the carpet.

So, it hadn't been a dream. Hunter had come in with her and they'd made love. Or maybe they'd just had sex. He certainly appeared to have made a fast exit. There was no note. Nothing.

Briana threw herself in the shower for a fast rinse-off. There was no time to wash her hair. She put on the sweater and jeans again, with fresh underwear, thrust the last few things in the bag and gathered her belongings.

In the meantime, her mind was searching for some kind of explanation for Hunter's behavior. He'd been such a gentleman. But leaving with no word, no pretense even of a future, almost destroyed her. Did he care nothing about her? Had she been so misled by his behavior that she'd completely misread his character?

She couldn't call his room and ask him because the only name she had was Hunter. She'd assumed that was his first name, but she didn't know.

She stared at the phone, tempted to try anyway, but she knew she didn't have time. She was going to have to chalk the bizarre night and even stranger morning to experience and go catch her plane.

As she stood in the doorway for a long moment, tears came to her eyes. She'd thought this morning she'd found something special. But like so many women, she'd been misled by a handsome face and broad shoulders. And a gentle touch and blue eyes to die for.

What a jerk!

HALF AN HOUR later, Hunter hurried down the stairs again. He was feeling much better, even though he still hadn't had much sleep. But he'd showered and shaved and changed into jeans and shirt, sports shoes, comfortable again. And he was looking forward to breakfast with Briana.

He hoped she'd gotten enough rest. It was just past eight-thirty, and he didn't want to wait too long to wake her up. His flight left at two, but he didn't know her schedule. He wanted to spend time with her before they had to be parted for however long it took for him to arrange his schedule. To work out their lives.

He shoved his hands in his pockets and started whistling as he reached her floor. It was a glorious day. When he'd arrived at the conference, he'd had a lousy attitude. He hadn't been happy lately. Now, he was on top of the world. One of the maids had her cart in the hallway near Briana's room, and Hunter greeted her cheerfully.

He passed her and reached Bri's room, and began to knock on the door. He hoped he could wake her. She slept so soundly.

"No one's there."

He whirled around, realizing it was the maid speaking.

Smiling, he explained, "No, she's there. She's a sound sleeper."

The maid shook her head. "No, they just called me from downstairs to clean the room. She checked out a few minutes ago."

The smile on his face disappeared. "No, you're wrong. She's still sleeping."

The maid shrugged her shoulders and turned away. Hunter formed a fist and beat on the door now, determined to awaken Briana.

"Here, I'll open the door."

He found the maid beside him, a look of sympathy on her face.

"Thanks. I'll wake her up."

He pushed into the room, only to find it empty. The bed with the sheets in disarray, the closet empty, nothing in the bathroom. No note.

"Where is she?" he demanded harshly, turning to the maid.

His expression must've frightened her because she backed up a step. "I told you. She checked out a few minutes ago."

"No, she wouldn't have just left! There's some mistake." He searched the room again for some mi-

nute piece of evidence that would tell him something—anything about Briana. But there was nothing.

"Sorry, sir." The maid stayed pressed against the
wall, trying to keep out of his way.

"Thanks," he managed as he left the room and ran
for the elevators. As soon as he reached the main
floor, he hurried over to the front desk. "A woman
named Briana, from room 812, just checked out?"

"Yes, sir. Miss McCallum left for the airport about
twenty minutes ago." The young man behind the
desk smiled, pleased to serve a customer properly.

"McCallum? Briana McCallum?"

"Yes, sir. I helped her myself."

Now why did that name sound familiar? Mc-
Callum. Then he remembered. Maitland Maternity
Hospital, the famous maternity hospital in Austin,
Texas, was opening a new wing, a state-of-the-art facility specializing in multiple births. The McCallum
Wing, dedicated to the donor's wife, who'd died in
childbirth. Administered by the donor's daughter. It
had been the main gossip of the conference, height-
ened by questions about her competency. Most everyone figured she was a rich woman playing at being a
do-gooder. He usually gave people the benefit of the
doubt, but he was in too much pain.

Briana McCallum. Rich woman. Looking for a new
thrill. How about a doctor? Try one for the night and
then skip town if it didn't work out?

But it did work out! He raged within himself. It

did! How could she deny what had happened between them? How could she just leave?

"Sir?" The clerk said with a frown. "Is anything wrong?"

"No!" Hunter snapped. "No, nothing's wrong."

What could be wrong? He asked himself savagely. He knew his lover's name now. Briana McCallum. A rich woman—who had walked away.

But she hadn't left her name for him. She hadn't wanted him to know. She hadn't wanted any more than what she'd got.

He hoped she was satisfied.

He wasn't.

Chapter Four

Seven months later

Briana McCallum was on the first floor of the new wing of Maitland Maternity Hospital, the McCallum Wing, dedicated to her mother, talking to the head of nursing, when the phone rang. Mrs. Rodgers interrupted their conversation to take the call, then handed the phone to Briana.

"It's for you."

Bri took the phone, expecting the caller to be her assistant. She wasn't disappointed. "What is it, Lisa?"

"The new doctor's here! R. J. Maitland wants you to come meet him at once."

"I thought he wasn't supposed to arrive until two o'clock," Bri complained. She hated all the politics involved in her job.

"He got here early. Come on. I told Mr. Maitland you'd be in his office in five minutes."

"All right. I'm on my way."

She struggled up from her chair as she handed the phone back to Mrs. Rodgers. "Okay, I think I've got a grasp of the problem, Mrs. Rodgers. I'll get back to you as soon as I've worked out a solution. But the new obstetrics chief for the wing has arrived early and I've got to go be a part of the welcoming committee."

"Oh!" Mary Rodgers said with excitement. "Dr. Callaghan? That's wonderful. I'm so looking forward to meeting him!"

Bri smiled tolerantly. She'd had nothing to do with choosing the new doctor, but she'd heard plenty of praise about him. Their head doctor, Dr. Wellborn, had collapsed with a heart attack ten days before the new wing opened. He was recovering, but he'd be unable to take up his appointment. Bri had had her hands full trying to make the adjustments necessary for everything to be up and running smoothly. She'd scarcely had time to note that a committee had hurriedly formed, much less looked at the candidates. She had her own fish to fry.

Now, having survived the opening, she could turn her attention to the newcomer. She sent up a prayer that the new man would be easy to work with. He should be. He'd have the best equipment and staff that money could buy.

It suddenly occurred to her that the reception she'd planned for that afternoon might need to be moved. Instead of heading for R. J. Maitland's office, she stopped by hers.

"Lisa? Did Mr. Maitland say—" She broke off as she realized her assistant's office was filled with people.

"Oh, here she is!" Lisa exclaimed, drawing her attention.

R. J. Maitland, director of the Maitland Maternity complex, stepped forward. "Bri, we gave up waiting for you. Here's Dr. Hunter Callaghan, waiting to meet you."

Bri actually felt the blood drain out of her face as she turned to look at the only man she'd ever known named Hunter.

That's the last thing she remembered.

DR. HUNTER CALLAGHAN, recently of Chicago, stared down at Briana McCallum, who'd just wilted onto the floor. Same beautiful hazel eyes, he'd noted before she'd closed them. Same silky light-brown hair framing her beautiful face. Same peaches-and-cream complexion, until all the blood had drained out of her face.

But there was a big difference between this Briana and the Briana he'd left sleeping in a hotel-room bed in New York City seven months ago.

This Briana was very definitely pregnant. Almost full-term, if he was any judge. So she'd been pregnant with another man's baby when he'd met her. She'd said she had no boyfriend, hadn't she? That she was alone? That was the impression he remembered. Obviously she was not only a wealthy woman, but a liar, too.

Dr. Abby Maitland McDermott, who was chief ob-gyn at Maitland Maternity and who had accompanied her brother R.J. and Hunter, bent over and took Bri's pulse as she chastised Lisa. "I told you to keep her from rushing around, Lisa. Having triplets carries enough pressure without adding to it."

Hunter stiffened. "She's having triplets?"

"Yeah, we're all excited that one of our first customers is our own administrator," Abby told him with a grin.

"How far along is she?" Hunter asked, a slight tremble in his voice that he hoped no one noticed.

"Help me lift her to the sofa. Everyone stand back and give her some room to breathe," Abby ordered.

Hunter stepped forward and put his hands on Briana. Lifting her shoulders, he slid his arm under her and lifted. Her head rolled over against his chest. As it had in the deli. Gently, he placed her on the sofa.

"She's seven months along and doing well. I don't know what caused today's fainting episode, but we'll check her out. Lisa, call and tell my staff I want a room for Bri."

"Oh, Doctor, she won't like that. Can't you wait until she comes to and ask her?" the assistant pleaded.

"No, I'm her doctor. I get to decide what kind of treatment she receives. Get a bed."

"Yes, ma'am," Lisa said.

"Don't get me a bed, Lisa," a faint voice Hunter had never forgotten spoke up. "I'm fine, Abby. You're right. I rushed because your brother is such a bear when he's kept waiting." Bri accompanied her words with a weak smile.

Hunter watched her, waiting to see if she remembered being introduced to him.

"I apologize for all the trouble, Dr. Callaghan. Not a particularly graceful way to welcome you to the McCallum Wing," she said in her soft voice, but Hunter noted she didn't look at him.

Swinging her feet off the sofa, she looked at R. J. Maitland. "I wanted to know if you want the reception set up for now, or leave it at two o'clock?"

"It can stay at two," the director said.

"But I'd really like to check you out, Bri," Abby said. "At twenty-eight weeks, you're doing well, but I'd like you to carry the girls a little longer."

"I intend to, Abby," she assured her, her smile sassier this time. "Now, I have a list of problems to deal with before the reception this afternoon, so if you and our new head of obstetrics will excuse me, I'll get busy." She smiled at the rest of the group, several other members of the Maitland family, and stood.

They all began to leave the office. Hunter, however, stood his ground. Finally, R. J. Maitland said, "Hunter, you coming?"

"I need a word with my new administrator," he said. A hazel-eyed gaze collided with his.

Abby stepped forward once again. "I'd rather Bri

not deal with much right now. In fact, though she said she was going to deal with problems, I'm ordering her back on the couch to rest.'' She smiled at Bri, and Hunter was filled with jealousy when Bri smiled back. Bri hadn't smiled at him that way.

"I just wanted to set up a time for a meeting with her," Hunter explained.

"Oh, Lisa? Does Bri have a time cleared to meet with Dr. Callaghan?" R.J. asked.

"She set aside some time tomorrow morning. She thought he might be too busy with the welcome until then."

"I knew Bri would have," R.J. said with a sigh. "She's so damned efficient it wears you out just thinking about it."

"Fine. I'll see you then, Ms. McCallum." Hunter said, trying to sound impersonal. But it wasn't easy. His mind was all ajumble. She could be carrying his child—children! He could go from bachelor to father of three in the space of a few weeks—if her babies were his.

He walked out of the office with R.J. "So she's having three girls? Fraternal?" He hoped R.J. would believe the huskiness of his voice was excitement about the new job.

"No, identical."

"Is her husband pleased?" He held his breath for Maitland's response.

"She's not married."

"But surely the babies' father is participating in the pregnancy," he pressed.

"She's never named anyone as father. Refuses to do so. Says these are her babies." R.J. changed the subject to the medical equipment available, and Hunter could do nothing but go along with him. Otherwise, it would've appeared odd.

But he hadn't seen the last of Briana McCallum today. And he suspected she knew it, too.

ONCE THE DOOR had closed behind her visitors, Briana slid back down to sit on the sofa before she fell on her face. Her knees were so wobbly, she knew she couldn't walk.

"Bri?" her assistant demanded, alarm in her voice. "Are you really sick? Do you need the hospital bed Dr. Abby asked for?"

"No, Lisa. But I could use a bottle of apple juice." She kept juice and nutrition bars in the small kitchen area beside her office. Lisa scurried away at once and returned with the apple juice.

"Are the girls all right?" she asked as she handed the juice to Briana.

"The girls are fine. Where is the file on Dr. Callaghan? I meant to read it before he arrived, and his early arrival has thrown me off." She hoped that excuse made sense to Lisa. "Could you bring it to me so I can review it while I'm catching my breath?"

Lisa scurried off to Bri's office to find the file on her desk and bring it back to her. Then, clutching the file and her juice, Bri stood. "I'm going to get into my rocker and study the file."

Lisa escorted her to the rocker in her office overlooking a spectacular view of Austin, and saw her settled. Then she asked if Bri needed anything else and assured her she should just call if she didn't feel well.

Gently, Bri smiled. "I know, Lisa. Thanks for taking such good care of me, but I'm fine." *Now that I've recovered from seeing the girls' daddy come through the door. What a shock.*

She'd actually thought she'd never see Hunter again. Some nights she'd prayed she'd never see him again. Others she'd prayed the opposite. The memory of their one time together still promised it would be heaven to be with him again. The anger and pain of his dismissal of her contradicted that thought.

What did he think? With any luck, he wouldn't realize he was the father. But Abby had been pretty specific about the length of her pregnancy. Maybe she could convince Hunter she'd gotten off the plane and been met by an old lover who'd begged her forgiveness. She examined that thought from several angles. How could he dispute it?

That's what she'd tell him. As long as she denied his involvement, he'd leave her alone. And that's what she wanted, she assured herself staunchly. To be left alone.

In the seven months since she'd left the hotel in New York, she'd adjusted to the changes in her life.

She was prepared for the birth of her children, three precious little girls. Her family was supportive, though Caleb still wanted to go beat up the father, whoever he was.

Her friends, too, at the hospital, never mentioned the fact that she was to be a single mother. They were happy for her. Everything was perfect.

Most of all, she was happy about her babies. Thrilled, in fact. She had enough money to eliminate a lot of the problems most single parents had. And she knew what her babies needed that money couldn't buy: love. Her babies would know she loved them. They'd know how special they were to her. Like she would have if her mother had lived. A shiver ran over her body. Yes, her girls would be loved.

And then along came Hunter Callaghan. What was he doing here? Obviously, he hadn't known who she was, that she was here, or he wouldn't have come. Or maybe he figured he shouldn't let his personal life interfere with his career. And being head of the McCallum Wing was a definite feather in his cap. There were only two or three comparative situations in the country.

Well, she could be professional. She'd deny his involvement with her pregnancy and continue as before.

Her mind drifted back to picture Hunter, standing there in his expensive suit, looking fit and handsome. Probably all the nurses had been drooling over him already. They'd certainly talked about the fact that he wasn't married.

Which reminded her of the file in her hands. She opened the folder and read through Hunter's impressive credentials. He was certainly qualified.

But she didn't want him to have anything to do with her babies' birth. Not even as an observer. He was to keep away. He'd walked out on her, left her alone in that hotel room without even asking her if she was okay. He'd broken her heart. She wasn't going to do the same thing to the girls.

"Is she all right?" Bri heard someone ask. Before she could react, Lisa opened the door to escort in one of Bri's best friends, Annabelle Reardon, a delivery nurse at Maitland.

"Of course I'm all right," Bri answered as they came in, but she didn't rise from her chair. Her friends didn't expect that these days.

"But gossip said you fainted," Annabelle said, alarm in her voice.

"Annabelle, you're being way too dramatic. I'm fine. See for yourself," Bri said, spreading her arms wide.

Taking her at her word, Annabelle pulled a chair over to the rocker and sat down to take Bri's pulse. Bri dismissed Lisa with a nod over Annabelle's shoulder.

"You know, you're acting like my mother, and I'm ten years older than you," Bri pointed out with a grin.

"Not ten years, Bri. You're exaggerating. Your

pulse is normal,'' she said as she put Bri's wrist back on the chair.

''Of course it is, because nothing's wrong. I just rushed a little too much because the great Dr. Callaghan got here early.''

''You don't like him?''

Bri warned herself to be careful. ''Of course, what little I know. I was referring to the nurses' enthusiasm for his, um, appearance.''

''You've heard the roar of appreciation?'' Annabelle asked with a grin. ''Mind you, I don't think he compares to our Dr. Beaumont.''

''Of course not. You've got a crush on him.''

"You've never said who—" Annabelle began and then broke off.

"No I haven't. And I won't. The man involved didn't want any future with me. These are my babies. No one else's."

"I know. I'm sorry." There was a moment of silence, as if Annabelle was remembering the past seven months. "How's Maggie?"

Bri sighed. "She's fine. Not pregnant." Her sister-in-law, Adam's wife, had been trying to get pregnant for some time. Her inability to conceive had put a real strain on her marriage. When Bri had announced her pregnancy, however, Maggie had been as supportive as a real sister. Just thinking about the courage and generosity Maggie had shown brought tears to her eyes.

"It's unfair," she whispered, closing her eyes.

"Maybe things will change soon," Annabelle said. "I didn't mean to upset you."

Bri forced her eyes open and pasted a smile on her face. "Oh, it's those hormones, Annabelle. You know how those affect us expectant mothers."

"Yeah. And anyway, Madeline's a miracle worker, so probably Maggie will have a baby before we know it."

Bri had believed that at first. Madeline Sheppard was one of the fertility experts at the McCallum Multiple Birth Wing. But so far, there were no results. Bri feared for Adam's marriage. Maggie seemed unable to think of anything else.

The door opened again and another friend, neonatal nurse April Sullivan rushed in. Instead of speaking to Bri, she looked at Annabelle. "Is she all right?"

Bri chuckled. "You'd think you'd ask me, silly," she said, reaching out for April's hand.

"She seems to be okay," Annabelle answered anyway.

"Okay, now that I've had a professional opinion, I'll ask you," April said to Bri, with a grin at Annabelle.

"Oh, you nurses! I'm fine, April. What are you doing here?"

"Well, word has flown all over the hospital that you fainted. You know how excited we all are about your babies. So I took a break to come make sure you're all right."

"Not all over the hospital?"

Both ladies nodded.

"Oh, no, that means I'll have a lot of visitors."

As if on cue, the door burst open and a handsome man, with hazel eyes just like Bri's, burst into the room. "Are you all right?" he demanded, ignoring her other guests.

Bri grinned at her younger—by three minutes—brother. "Of course I am. I just tried to hurry too much. How did you hear?"

Though he'd at least asked *her* first, Caleb now looked at the other two women. "I was running an errand for Dad. Is she telling the truth?"

"Caleb!" Bri protested, still grinning. It wouldn't

have been the first time she'd tried to con her brothers, and they both knew it.

"As far as we can tell. Abby was there, and she seemed to think everything was fine," April said.

"All right," Caleb said with a sigh.

Bri relaxed again, glad her brother was satisfied. Until he spoke again.

"I'll be back around five to take you home. I don't want you driving anymore. I'll bring you to work each day and take you home."

"You'll do no such thing. I am not an invalid. I'm pregnant, that's all. I'm perfectly capable of driving a car."

"Bri, you'll do as you're told," he ordered in his sternest voice. It wasn't the first time he'd tried to give Bri orders.

"I'll do as my doctor orders me, dear brother, and Abby assures me I should continue to lead a normal life until she says differently."

"But I did tell you to rest, didn't I?" Abby said from behind Caleb. "How can you rest with the room full of people?"

"Abby, don't tell me you've taken time to come back and check on me," Bri protested.

"Yes, and it's a good thing. Everybody out. I want my patient to rest. Lisa is going to bring you your lunch, Bri. I don't want you traipsing down to the cafeteria. In fact, I want you in that chair or on the sofa from now until two when you'll have to make an appearance at the welcoming party."

"But Abby, I'll need to make sure my directions are being carried out before it starts," Bri protested.

"Send Lisa. I mean it, Bri. Either you cooperate or I put you in that hospital bed."

Bri sighed and looked at her brother and friends. "Okay, guys, I guess you'd better go. Oh, Abby, tell Caleb I can still drive myself to work," she asked hurriedly as her brother was turning toward the door.

He paused and stared at Abby.

After looking at first Caleb and then Bri, Abby said, "For now, she can still drive herself to work."

Caleb frowned, but gave an abrupt nod and left the room. The two nurses followed, with offers to do anything for Bri thrown over their shoulders.

Finally, with only Abby in the room, the doctor moved to her side and picked up her wrist.

"Annabelle already checked my pulse."

"Good for her," Abby said mildly, continuing to watch her wristwatch.

Bri shook her head in disgust. "Well?"

"Your pulse is fine. But I do have a question for you."

"Sure. I ate breakfast, I promise, and I've taken it easy."

"I know you have. What I don't know is why you fainted at the sight of Dr. Hunter Callaghan."

Chapter Five

"I—I guess I hurried too much when Lisa called me. You know how your brother is about wanting everything to run smoothly."

"Don't give me that garbage about R.J. scaring you. I've seen you go toe-to-toe with him when you think he's wrong."

Bri thought desperately. "I have several problems I need to deal with. I guess I went on overload. I don't have as big a capacity for trouble right now."

Abby stared at her a little longer. Then she reached over and felt Bri's cheeks, as if she were a mother checking her child for fever.

"Is your back hurting?"

"No, not at all."

"Are you having any pains anywhere?"

"None, other than when one of the girls gets under my ribs and gives me a swift kick." There wasn't a lot of room for three babies, even with her stomach as big as it was.

"Hmmm." Abby continued to stare. Finally, she

said, "Okay, but if you have any pain, no matter how minor, you have Lisa page me, you hear?"

"I hear, Abby, and I will. I won't take any chances with my girls. You know that."

"I know. And that's the only reason I'm letting you stay out of a hospital bed. I want you to lead a normal life as long as you can. I believe that helps the health of the babies."

"Me, too," Bri agreed, giving Abby her best smile. "Emily, Elizabeth and Eleanor are going to be the healthiest triplets ever born."

"Okay. So follow my orders until two o'clock. You can put in a brief appearance at the welcoming party, but don't stay long."

"I won't. I promise." Relieved that she'd have a good excuse to exit early, her smile grew even brighter.

"Then I'll see you there. And eat all your lunch!"

"Yes, ma'am." Bri even added a mock salute as Abby left her office.

Alone once again, Bri released a big sigh. She hadn't even gotten around to worrying about the welcoming party. Before she could, Abby had given her an out. She'd go for the initial introduction, shake Hunter's hand...dear heavens, she didn't want to touch him.

"You're being ridiculous!" she exclaimed to herself. Their brief acquaintance had happened seven months ago. She'd simply exaggerated the effect he had on her. That was all, a silly exaggeration. She could shake his hand, as if they were two business acquaintances, without feeling anything. Nothing to it.

She drew a deep breath.

"Did you call me?" Lisa asked from the door.

"Uh, no, I hate to admit it, but I was talking out loud to the girls. Sorry."

"No problem. I think that's so sweet. They're lucky girls to have you for a mom."

Bri smiled at her assistant. "Thanks, Lisa. You always make me feel better."

"I'm going down now to get your lunch. I've switched the phones to voice mail, so don't bother answering them. Just stay in your rocker and rest."

"I promise to follow orders," she agreed, and Lisa nodded, disappearing from view.

And the best thing she could do for herself and her girls was not to think about the new obstetrics chief for the McCallum Wing. Ever. She didn't want her girls feeling any connection to the man.

They were her daughters. Three little miracles who belonged to no one else. That was her story and she was sticking to it!

HUNTER FOLLOWED R. J. Maitland through the wing, impressed with the facilities and the friendliness of the staff. He wouldn't find out about their skills until he saw them in action.

"You're cutting a wide swath through our nursing staff," R.J. muttered as they left yet another area.

Hunter frowned. "What do you mean?"

"You haven't noticed all the younger nurses fainting at your feet? Even some of the older ones are swooning."

Hunter continued to stare at him, wondering what he was talking about.

"Man, the nurses are interested. Surely you noticed?"

"Look, Maitland, all I've seen are a lot of friendly faces, which I appreciate. I think you're exaggerating."

"I thought you were single."

"I am. Very."

"Not looking?"

Hunter ground his teeth together, wondering what the man would say if he told him he'd learned his lesson about women at his administrator's hands. Instead, he said simply, "No, I'm not looking." Then, before the man could speak, he added, "And, before you ask, I'm not gay. I'm just intent on my work."

"Good enough. I hope if you do decide to, uh, change your status, you'll look outside the hospital. I'm sure local Austin society will make you feel welcome. Some of our Texas ladies are real lookers."

Hunter smiled. He'd already heard stories about Maitland Maternity's past history. "Like you looked outside the hospital?"

R. J. Maitland's cheeks turned bright red. He cleared his throat. "Well, uh, I guess you know I didn't.'' R.J. had married his secretary Dana Dillinger.

"Yeah, I know. But I didn't let it sway my decision to come here. I don't think personal relationships affect a man's work that much."

"Okay. Let me take you to your office now. You already have an assistant, Mrs. Helen Robb. If you don't think you can work with her, let me know. I'll find another place for her and you can hire your own assistant."

"Thanks. I'll let you know." Hunter hoped he could work with the woman, but if she was young and followed him around all day long, he'd take R.J. up on his offer. He wanted nothing to do with romance or women.

But he did want to talk to Briana.

Not because he was still attracted to her. He'd explained away his attraction a million times. When he'd let down his guard over the past seven months and found himself yearning for her, he'd immediately reminded himself that she was a wealthy woman, looking for kicks, taking a title to make herself feel important.

Not the woman for him.

But for those few hours when he'd held her, when he'd made love to her, she'd been his dream, his future, his love. He was fortunate, really, that she'd slapped him in the face with reality so quickly. If he'd spent a month or two believing in that fantasy, he might not be able to dismiss those thoughts so easily.

He ignored the sarcastic laughter those thoughts earned from his mind. He was beginning to think he'd misjudged Briana because he was afraid of being hurt. He'd sought ways to dismiss the magic of their time together to make it easier to forget her.

"Hunter? Allow me to introduce Mrs. Helen Robb," R.J. said, jolting him from his thoughts. Apparently they'd reached his office while he was thinking. He had no idea how they'd gotten here.

"Welcome to Maitland Maternity, and McCallum Wing in particular, Dr. Callaghan."

Hunter stared at the trim, gray-haired woman. Her voice was serene and soothing. Now, if she had brains, he was in luck.

"Thank you, Mrs. Robb."

"Please, call me Helen. Everyone does." She turned and led the way into his office. "I arranged the furniture to my liking. If there's anything you want changed, don't hesitate to tell me. I'll call maintenance and get someone up here at once."

His office was large. "I like the arrangement very much. It looks efficient and soothing." The decor was done in blue and beige with an occasional touch of yellow.

"I left room on the wall by the windows for your degrees and certificates. If you'll give them to me when you've unpacked, I'll see that they are hung in place."

"Perfect. Have you worked at the hospital long?"

"Yes, almost since the beginning. I was Mr. William Maitland's secretary until he died. Then I've worked in different departments, so I feel I know the hospital well.''

Hunter looked at R.J. and nodded before he responded to her words. ''Good. You'll be a big help to me as I try to learn everyone's name and position. Thank you, Helen.''

She smiled and disappeared into the outer office.

''She seems perfect, R.J. Thanks.''

''She's one of the best. But if a problem arises, let me know. Now, do you want to go to lunch at a nearby restaurant, eat in the cafeteria, skip lunch while you settle in, have Helen bring you something, or—''

''I'd love for Helen to bring me something while I get settled in, if that wouldn't be rude of me. I'm anxious to find my footing. Everything happened so quickly, I need some time. It's only been ten days since I first interviewed.''

''Of course, and Helen will be glad to do so. She'll start you a tab in the cafeteria. You don't pay until after you've run up a hundred dollars a month, so you don't have to give her any money,'' he added as Hunter reached for his wallet. ''It's part of your contract.''

''Maybe the first thing I'd better do is read the details on that contract,'' Hunter said with a laugh. ''I'd forgotten that little benefit.''

R.J. smiled in return. ''I'm just glad you signed it. You could've stayed in Chicago and received the

same promotion within another year. We feel fortunate you felt like a change of venue. Any particular
reason?''

Hunter avoided the other man's gaze. With a shrug
of his shoulders, he said, ''You know, sometimes you
just feel the need to move on. And Maitland Maternity Hospital, even without the new wing, has a great
reputation.''

''True. Well, welcome one more time. I'll stop by
at two and pick you up for your welcoming party.''

''Thanks,'' Hunter said again. Once R. J. Maitland,
whom Hunter liked so far, had disappeared he
breathed a sigh of relief. No more questions about his
acceptance of the job. He didn't want his reasons examined too closely. He didn't even want to think
about them. After telling himself he didn't ever want
to see her again, he'd jumped at the chance to work
with her. The job was a good one, but Briana had
been the deciding factor.

When Helen appeared at his door after he called
her name, he asked her to fetch him lunch. She gave
him a succinct summation of what they offered, and
he chose randomly and sent her on her way.

Now he was really alone.

No one watching, no one talking, no one guessing
about him.

Now he could replay his meeting with a very pregnant Briana McCallum. Pregnant with his children.
He was going to be a father of three identical little
girls. At least he thought so. He'd dreamed of having

a family—one day. When he'd found Briana seven months ago, he'd dreamed of the family they would have. But then reality had slapped him in the face. He wasn't married, making a future.

Reality. What would she expect of him? Now that she knew how to find him, would she insist on marriage?

His heart sped up as he again remembered the sensations he'd felt when he'd held her in his arms. Sensations he'd dismissed for seven months. They weren't so easily dismissed now.

But he didn't dare give in to those thoughts. He still had no proof that Briana was anything but a rich uncaring woman. She probably had no intention of raising her children. Maybe she was like her father, not interested in babies.

Even he couldn't believe that fantasy. She might have left him high and dry. She might not have been interested in a future with him. But he'd seen nothing in their brief time together that said she would ignore her—their daughters.

And he intended to play a role in his daughters' lives, so if she insisted on marriage, then he'd marry her. He didn't want anyone calling his daughters illegitimate. He'd punch their lights out if they dared.

So, a marriage of convenience?

That was probably what she'd want. He could handle that. Of course he could. He began massaging his temples at the thought of living in the same house with Briana and never touching her. Never.

"Dr. Callaghan? Do you have a headache?" Helen asked. She'd entered his office quietly while his eyes were closed.

"No! No, not at all. I was thinking. That was fast, Helen. I promise I won't ask you to wait on me all the time. I just needed a little time to myself."

"I don't mind at all."

"Have you eaten?"

"I picked myself up some lunch while I was there."

"Why don't you bring it in here and we can talk while we eat. Unless you would be uncomfortable?"

"Not at all."

Hunter wondered how long it would take him to lead the conversation to Briana McCallum without being obvious. Because she was the only part of the hospital he was interested in right now.

At FIVE UNTIL TWO, Briana touched up her makeup, determined not to look washed out, combed her hair, smoothed any wrinkles out of her navy blue two-piece maternity suit, and started out of her office for the welcoming party in the cafeteria.

"Are you ready to go, Bri?" Lisa asked, jumping up from her desk. "Dr. Abby said I was to go with you, in case you felt faint."

Bri sighed. She was paying a heavy price for her silly fainting spell. But it wouldn't happen again. Because she wasn't going to be surprised again. "Fine, Lisa." She waited patiently for Lisa to reach her side.

"The new doctor sure is a looker. Everyone's talking about how handsome he is. You should hear all the nurses."

Bri sank her teeth into her bottom lip. It shouldn't bother her. She already knew he was handsome. But she also knew he was one of those men who took his pleasure and avoided the consequences. He was a jerk, plain and simple.

"Really? I guess I didn't notice his appearance all that much."

Lisa giggled. "I guess not. You were too busy fainting." Then she covered her lips with her free hand. "Oops, sorry, Bri."

"Nothing to be sorry about. That about sums it up. So, did you think he was that handsome?"

"Wow, yeah! I mean, I guess he's too old for me, but he's very handsome. And he has just a few grey hairs at his temples. They blend in with his blond hair, but still, they make him look distinguished. I'd trust him with my life," she added, a dreamy expression on her face.

"Good looks aren't a lot of help in a medical emergency, Lisa," Bri pointed out, sarcasm in her voice.

"I know, but what I meant is he looks trustworthy."

"Even jerks can look trustworthy. That's why they get the opportunity to be a jerk. No one trusts an ugly man."

"That's not true. I trust Benny, and he's not handsome."

"I trust Benny, too, and I think he's kind of cute."
Lisa giggled. "Yeah, so do I."

Benny was a paramedic who made deliveries to the
hospital. Sometimes he and his partner would go to
the cafeteria and have a cup of coffee. His nose
looked as if it had been broken, and he could use a
good dentist, but he had a heart of gold.

They'd arrived at the cafeteria, and Briana immediately began checking to see if everything had been
done as she'd asked. The cafeteria supervisor appeared at her side to see if there was anything else to
be done.

"It looks wonderful, Mrs. C.," Bri said at once.

Joanna Carpenter beamed at her. "Oh, thanks, Bri.
I think I did everything you asked. Come have a look
at the cake. Sam did a great job decorating it. He's
getting very good."

Bri looked at the cake and offered praise for Sam,
the baker in their cafeteria. It hadn't been an easy task
writing Welcome Dr. Callaghan on the cake.

Members of the staff began filling the cafeteria,
many of them checking on Bri before they drifted off
to chat with friends.

When the new arrival entered with R. J. Maitland,
a cheer went up from everyone gathered, and helium
balloons were released from bags in several corners
of the room. Of course, they didn't have far to go but
soon the strings tied on them were hanging down,
allowing those present to take one of them as a sou-
venir. And they did add a lot of color.

R. J. Maitland raised one hand for silence and again welcomed Hunter Callaghan, obstetrician extraordinaire to the staff, adding an impressive list of qualifications. Everyone cheered again when he'd finished and began shouting for Dr. Callaghan to speak.

Hunter nodded, smiled and held his hand up in appreciation for their welcome. When they quieted, he made a gracious speech about how much he was looking forward to working with them and how much he appreciated the warmth of their welcome.

Bri tried to ignore the warm tendrils of remembrance that curled around her heart as she listened to his voice. How calming that voice had been when they were stuck in the storeroom. How exciting it had been when he'd held her in his arms and made love to her.

Now it meant nothing to her, she assured herself. Nothing at all. But she didn't approach him at once to excuse herself. She had to have time to regain control, because touching him could be even worse than hearing his voice.

Finally, she approached the table where he was eating his piece of cake and assuring Sam it was the best cake he'd ever had. Sam, beaming, backed away from the table and Bri just barely managed to sidestep him in time.

"Oh, Bri! I'm so sorry! I didn't hurt you, did I?"

"No, Sam, not at all."

"Did you get a piece of cake?"

"I'd love one, but my doctor said I had to give up all that sugar for a while."

"Oh, of course. When you can eat cake again, I'll bake you a special one."

"I'll hold you to that."

Sam kissed her cheek and hurried off to the kitchen where he could repeat Hunter's appreciative remarks to his friends.

Dr. Callaghan, as she was determined to think of him, had risen to his feet and stood waiting.

Bri kept about three feet of distance between her and the table. "Sorry to interrupt, R.J., Dr. Callaghan. I wanted to welcome you again to our wing, Dr. Callaghan. And to excuse myself. Abby insisted I only stay a couple of minutes."

R.J. stood and crossed the three feet and kissed her on the cheek. "You did a bang-up job, Bri. Now go take care of those girls. I'm sure Hunter agrees that their well-being takes precedence over any party."

"Thanks, R.J." She immediately turned to head for the door, but she couldn't escape quite so quickly.

"Ms. McCallum," Hunter said, stopping her in her tracks. "Thanks for arranging such a nice party."

"You're welcome," she said, backing up.

"And I believe you said you'd set aside some time in the morning for us to talk?"

Her gaze flickered to his blue eyes and hurriedly looked away. There was an edge to his words, almost threatening. "Yes, at nine in the morning, but only if you want to talk then. If you have more important things to do, we can make it when it's more convenient for you.''

"More convenient for me? Hmm, I'll let you know in the morning. Is that all right with you?''

"Yes, of course. Just let Lisa know.''

She hesitated, wanting to leave but not wanting to appear rude. That would start all kinds of rumors flying through the hospital. And endless questions.

Though she kept her gaze down, she couldn't help but see the hand he held out. Oh, my. She was going to have to shake his hand after all. Maybe she could claim to have poison ivy! Or the measles. Or—or— nothing else occurred to her. And none of her ideas would work. Abby would be all over her if she heard her say any of those silly things.

Come on, Briana, where's your courage? Just shake his hand and get out of here! She drew a deep breath and reached out to receive his offer of a handshake. It had to be her nerves that caused the trembling, not his flesh. But something happened. She felt like static electricity had shot through her.

With a gasp, she jerked her hand away and fled from Dr. Hunter Callaghan's presence. She'd think up a good excuse later...if anyone bothered to ask.

...

Chapter Six

When five o'clock rolled around, Lisa stuck her head
through the door. "It's time to go home, Bri. Are you
ready?"

"Not today, Lisa. It's been such a strange day, I
need a few more minutes to work before I can leave."

"But Dr. Abby said—"

"I know. But she said my life should go on as
normal for as long as I can manage it. And I definitely
wouldn't leave all this paperwork for tomorrow. Besides, I'm just going to sit here, no strain. I promise."
She gave Lisa her best smile. After all, she was the
boss.

"Okay, but maybe you should sleep in in the morning and come in late."

"And keep Dr. Callaghan waiting? Not a good career move." Bri would prefer to do as Lisa said, but
she knew she couldn't.

"Oh, I'd forgotten. Okay, but don't stay late."

"I won't." She looked down at the papers on her
desk, hoping Lisa would take the hint and leave with-

out more warnings. She appreciated all the concern from her colleagues, but she didn't need a hundred mother hens.

"'Night," Lisa called, and then there was silence.

She was alone at last. No more questions about her reaction to Dr. Callaghan's handshake. As she'd figured, there had been a few. She'd told them all it was carpet shock or something. Amazingly enough, they'd believed her. Or appeared to, even Abby, who'd dropped by around three to check on her.

Now, she'd passed all the tests and would probably only see the man at rare intervals. They could handle most of their business over the phone. She'd just have to deal with his voice.

She turned her attention back to her work. She only had a few minutes worth, but she wanted to make sure she didn't run into the good doctor as he left the building. She figured he'd be gone soon. After all, it was his first day. He couldn't be behind so quickly.

After she finished the last of her chores, she cleared her desk and made a list of what she needed to deal with when she first arrived in the morning. It was best not to be caught unawares.

A noise in Lisa's office caught her attention. "Is someone out there?" Briana called through the open door.

"Oh," Dr. Hunter Callaghan said as he appeared in the doorway. "You're still here. Good." He entered her office and closed the door behind him. "I thought we should have a little talk."

Briana struggled to control the panic welling up in her. "I was about to go home, Dr. Callaghan."

"Don't be so formal, Bri. Make it Hunter."

"I realize I said we'd talk at your convenience, Dr. Callaghan," she began, ignoring his offer of informality, "but I really think tomorrow morning would be better."

"Oh, we'll talk tomorrow morning. But that will be a business meeting. Right now I think we need to have a personal meeting."

He wasn't going to play the game. Pretend they'd never met. Okay, she'd take the gloves off. "Why? It's a little late to explain why you dumped me."

"Why I what?"

She lifted her chin, not about to be intimidated by his behavior. "Why you left me asleep and disappeared, no note, no nothing."

"Lady, I went to my room to shower and change. Then I came back down to take you to breakfast."

She sneered at him. "Easy to say, now, isn't it? Look, doctor, I prefer that we forget what happened in the past and simply work together as business colleagues, nothing more, nothing less." She shoved back her chair. "If you'll excuse me, now that we've got that straight, I'll be on my way."

"There's one problem with your suggestion," he said softly, glaring at her.

"What?"

"You're having my children." His blue eyes were

piercing, leaving her no—what had he called it?—wiggle room.

But she'd prepared for this moment. "You're wrong. I'm not having your children."

"Abby said you're twenty-eight weeks. That's exactly how long it's been since I made love to you in New York City."

She cleared her throat. "I realized it might seem that way to you, but then you don't know what happened when I got off the plane." She held her gaze steady, determined to do the best acting job of her life.

"What happened?"

"My ex-boyfriend met my plane. He convinced me that he was ready for commitment, which was what we argued over. I gave him a second chance. We were together about six weeks when I took a pregnancy test. Abby told me I was four weeks pregnant, she thought. You know how inexact these things can be."

"So where is he?"

"He panicked and ran. He wasn't ready after all." She sat silently, watching him, hoping and praying she'd convinced him.

"Have you told him about the girls?"

"No."

"Are you going to?"

"Why would I? He doesn't want any children. Why would we want him?"

"What's his name?"

She was tempted to make up a name, but she refrained. "I don't think that's any of your business, Dr. Callaghan. I haven't told anyone his name, and I don't intend to start now."

He stared at her and she fought to keep her gaze level to his.

"I'm prepared to marry you," he said abruptly, leaving her without anything to say.

When she didn't respond, he said, "I assumed that's what you would want, now that you know how to locate me."

She leaned back in her chair and lifted her chin another inch. "You're wrong, Dr. Callaghan. I'm not carrying your children, and I don't require such a sacrifice of you. You made your feelings toward me and any commitment quite clear that day in New York City when you disappeared."

"I told you, I was coming back. Of course, then I thought you were a working stiff, like me. Not the incredibly wealthy Ms. McCallum, hiding behind a title."

Bri tried to remember the need to keep her blood pressure down. Drawing several deep breaths, she counted to ten. Several times. Finally, she said, "You may not care for me personally, Dr. Callaghan, but I will not accept such disparaging remarks about my work."

"So I've heard. All people have done is praise your work. They always mention how hard you work, how efficient you are. I figured you shoveled all of it to your assistant's shoulders. They've assured me that's not true.''

She gave silent thanks for the support she'd received. She'd worked hard to ensure that no one thought she was taking an easy ride because of her name. ''I hope you're satisfied, then.'' She'd discovered the hard way that people assumed wealth meant no work on her part. That she would snap her fingers and get what she wanted.

''Not yet. I like to see things for myself.''

''I understand. And if I don't meet your standards, I'll expect you to let me know.''

''You can be sure of that. Are these my babies?''

She stared at the sudden switch of topic again. ''No, these are *my* babies, no one else's. Now, if you've finished with your questioning, I'd like to go home and rest.'' She'd like to get away from him, so she could relax. The tension was getting to her.

He stood, but instead of leaving, he came around the desk and began taking her pulse.

''What are you doing? You're not my doctor. I don't want you—''

''It's high. Are you on any medication for high blood pressure?''

''No! And my blood pressure will go down as soon as you leave!''

''How far away do you live?''

''That's none of your business. Go away!''

He smiled, which, seven months ago, would've

melted all her resistance. She was made of sterner stuff now.

"I can't let you drive with such high blood pressure. I'll drive you home." He took hold of her arm as if he intended to pull her to her feet.

"Turn me loose. I can stand by myself."

He lifted his hands, as if surrendering, and stood silently watching her.

Just what she wanted. Her ex-lover to see how awkward she was. "When you leave."

"I beg your pardon?"

"I'll stand when you leave." She sat in her chair, glaring at him.

"I'm afraid that's not acceptable. I can carry you, I can call an ambulance, or I can call your doctor. You may choose which option you prefer. Or you can stand now and we can walk out to my car."

She felt herself begin to shake, knowing she was pushing her limits. It was time for her to eat, too. Abby had explained the importance of eating regularly. Without saying anything, she stood. Then she bent over to pick up her bag. As she walked to the office door, she was aware of him following her, his tall form leaning protectively toward her.

Even on the nights when she'd hated him, she hadn't forgotten how protective he'd been—until he walked out on her. She made it to the elevator without him touching her, which was a major accomplishment. But it took a lot of energy to control her reaction.

It didn't take long to go down one floor. When the door opened, Hunter took one of her arms.

"You're trembling!" he exclaimed. "Are you all right?"

"It's time for me to eat. I'll fix something as soon as I drive home."

"You're not driving home. I'm driving you. But there's a café right here. Let's grab some dinner there before I take you home."

Bri debated her choices. If she ate, she should be able to drive home by herself. That would be better than this man taking her home. She opted for the Austin Eats Café, a favorite place of hers. "I'll go eat at the café. You don't have to join me. After I eat I'll be okay."

"We'll see," he said mildly, keeping hold of her arm. "Besides, I don't like to eat alone."

"Dr. Callaghan, you're being outrageous," she protested.

He pulled open the door to the restaurant. She saw several people she knew, since many of the staff at Maitland Maternity hung out at the diner. She could protest and they'd come to her aid, but how would that look? If she acquiesced to his company, everyone would think she was welcoming the new obstetrics chief.

"A lot of hospital people eat here. Unless you want to start rumors, we'd better pretend to be friendly."

"Why, Bri, we *are* friendly," he assured her with that lopsided smile, one that she'd never forgotten.

"Bri, how are you?" one of the waitresses called as she saw her enter. "Come on in. We've got a vacant booth back here."

Bri cringed as she knew what was coming next. She'd dined in here just recently.

The waitress pulled the table between the two bench seats all the way to one side. Then she looked at Hunter. "You don't mind sharing the same side with Bri, do you? She needs more room than most people these days."

"I'd be delighted to sit beside her," he said with a smile that had the waitress fluffing her hair. "Thank you."

"Glad to be of service. What can I bring you to drink while you're reading the menu?"

"I'll have ice water, please," Bri said before the waitress forgot she even existed. Hunter had that effect on women.

"Coffee for me," he said, then added, "Decaf if you have it."

"Sure do. I'll be right back."

After the waitress hurried away, Hunter leaned back and surveyed the diner. "Nice place. Very attentive service."

Bri rolled her eyes. "Duh. I wonder why?"

"Because you look like you're about to give birth at any minute?" he said, smiling down at her.

She looked away. "No. Because the waitress can't resist your smile."

"Some women manage."

It was on the tip of her tongue to point out that if she'd been able to do so, she wouldn't look like a blimp ready to pop. But then she remembered that he would realize she was carrying his children. And she didn't want that. She wasn't going to let a heartless man into her life. He might hurt her babies.

She flipped open the menu, though she practically knew it by heart. Not that she could order her favorite things right now. The girls didn't like the chili or the enchiladas she loved.

"What's good?" Hunter asked.

She pointed out several of her favorites, but when the waitress came to take their orders, she asked for baked chicken breast and steamed vegetables. Hunter asked for chicken-fried steak and french fries, preceded by a salad.

"You're a medical professional and you're going to eat those unhealthy things?" she prodded, irritated that he could and she couldn't.

He understood completely. "Don't worry. Not much longer and you can eat them, too."

She sighed and was so tempted to lean her head on his strong shoulders that she stiffened.

"So, how long are you planning on working?"

She looked up in surprise. "I'm going home. I said I would."

"No, I mean, how long before you go on maternity leave?"

"I'm going on maternity leave when I go into labor.'' Her voice was crisp, as if there was no room for discussion.

He frowned at her. ''Are you sure that's wise?''

''My doctor and I have discussed my decision and she agrees with me. And it's none of your business.'' He acted as though he should have a vote in her decision. She hadn't seen the man in seven months. Even then she'd only spent seven or eight hours with him.

''Maybe not, but as a medical professional—''

''Don't expect me to bow down. I work with medical professionals every day. While I respect your work, that does not make you God!''

The waitress returned with their food. She also brought a glass of milk. ''I forgot, Dr. Abby said for you to drink milk at every meal. Remember? Shelby says it's on the house,'' she added with a smile before heading back to the kitchen.

''Nice place,'' Hunter said without actually commenting on the milk. ''Who is Shelby?''

Briana took another deep breath. She'd planned to have her glass of milk at bedtime, but she guessed she'd have it now. Sometimes she thought everyone in Austin intended to supervise her babies' arrival. ''She's the owner of the diner, and sort of family to the Maitlands.''

''Sort of?''

''They're like cousins.''

''Okay.'' Then, as if they were really friends, he began telling her about his day, very innocuous stories that began to soothe her without her even realizing it. If anyone had said she'd share dinner with Hunter Callaghan and enjoy it, she'd have laughed in their faces. Especially about ten o'clock this morning.

By the time she'd finished her milk, vegetables and chicken, Hunter had cleaned his plate. "Very good food. I can tell I'll be eating here often," he said with a smile.

"Not much of a cook?"

"I can manage, but usually I put in long hours and I'm just too tired to want to cook. I suspect that happens to you, too. Everyone I talked to today mentioned what long hours you worked."

"Not lately. Abby's pretty strict with me."

"Good. I want my girls taken care of."

He said those words so casually, as if they both knew these babies were his. But she'd told him they weren't. "These are not your girls! They're mine. All mine."

"You shouldn't be so greedy, Bri. You're getting three. Surely you can share." His smile had a teasing tilt to it, but Bri didn't see anything to laugh about.

"I told you you're not the father!"

"A little louder and the rumors will be flying tomorrow."

He was right. She had forgotten where she was. And she was letting him upset her again. She drew another deep breath. "I need to go home now."

"As soon as I pay, we can go."

"I can pay for my meal, Doctor. And I don't need you to see me home. I'm perfectly fine now."

He gave her a steady look before saying, "Okay, you can drive home. I'll just follow you to be sure you get there all right."

"Ohhh! You're worse than Caleb!"

"Who's Caleb?" he demanded sharply.

"My baby brother. He thought he should start driving me back and forth from work. But Abby assured him I could manage a while longer."

The waitress came over to offer dessert, but Hunter gave her his credit card instead, saying they needed to go.

She rushed away, anxious to impress the doctor with her efficiency before Bri even protested.

She pulled a ten-dollar bill out of her purse and shoved it at him. "I said I'd pay for my meal."

To her surprise, he accepted the ten and folded it, stuffing it in his dress shirt pocket. "Okay, Miss Independent. Ready?" he asked as the waitress had him sign the receipt. Then he slid out of the booth and offered her a hand.

She started to refuse his help just to be rude, but it wasn't easy to slide out of the booth with both her and the girls, so she let him help her.

She was startled, however, when he wrapped an arm around her shoulders. "What do you think you're doing?" she whispered urgently.

"Escorting you home, just as I said," he responded, as if his behavior was normal.

"Take your arm down!" she urged, still whispering, not wanting to make a scene in front of people she knew.

"I just thought you could use a little support." He immediately did as she requested, however, which pacified her.

When they got outside, she said, "I didn't mean to be rude, but tomorrow there will already be a lot of talk about us eating together. If you appear too friendly, they'll think—never mind. Let's just keep our dealings on a business level."

"Yes, ma'am."

"Well, thank you for—for having dinner with me. I'll see you around nine, when it's convenient."

"Right."

She started off in the direction of her car, but he didn't move away. Instead, he fell into step beside her.

"What are you doing?" she demanded.

"Walking you to your car."

"I told you that's not necessary."

"Honey, even if you weren't pregnant with triplets, my mother would disagree with you. She was very strict about how we treated women, my brother and me. I have no choice, or she'll never let me sleep tonight."

She remembered him mentioning his mother when she'd suggested he sit and she stand in the storeroom. "Well, I certainly wouldn't want your sleep to be interrupted tonight!" she snapped.

"I knew you wouldn't," he agreed with a smile. "Do your feet swell these days?"

She considered telling him it was none of his business, but it seemed simpler to just say, "Yes."

"When we get to your place, I'll give you a foot massage. I'm pretty good at those."

As heavenly as that sounded, and only a very pregnant woman would appreciate the sacrifice she now made, she refused his offer.

"Don't worry," he said, as if she hadn't spoken, "I enjoy giving foot massages. Maybe I have a foot fetish. You can give me your opinion afterward."

He was teasing her and she knew it. She wanted to laugh and tease him back, but the last time she'd decided to quit trying to be strong and lean on Hunter, she'd ended up pregnant. Not something she wanted to try a second time. He'd broken her heart once. She wasn't going to risk her heart—or her girls—again. She'd been raised to be strong, to compete with her brothers. She mustn't forget.

When they reached her car, she said, "Thanks again for the escort. I'll see you in the morning."

"Now, honey, quit trying to ignore the foot thing. My car just happens to be right over there. If you'll wait just a minute, I'll be right behind you. We'll soon have you with happy feet, I promise."

Bri gave him a sweet smile, unlocked her car door and slid behind the wheel, grateful for her long legs that allowed her to still reach the pedals with the seat

pushed all the way back. She smiled again as Hunter
waved and headed toward his car.

Then she started the engine, threw her car in re-
verse and backed out of the parking spot. Putting the
car in drive, she peeled rubber out of the parking lot,
determined that the hardheaded man who'd been her
shadow for the past hour wouldn't be able to follow
her home.

Chapter Seven

Hunter stood in the parking lot, staring as Bri drove away.

He was an idiot. He'd offered to marry the woman, and she'd refused. So why did he still feel protective, concerned, mesmerized by her? He'd intended to keep his distance, not to risk his heart. But two minutes alone with her and he wanted to give her a foot rub.

He was crazy. But he wasn't going to walk away from his children. The girls, as Bri called them, would know their father. Briana might refuse to marry him, but he would claim his children. He'd have DNA tests run after their births if he had to. He would have his family with or without Briana.

Okay, so she wasn't a useless woman, wanting the glory without the work. Everyone had praised her work ethic. The McCallum Wing was functioning well. And that didn't happen without a good administrator. But a good work ethic didn't mean she was honorable in her dealings with men. Maybe she got her kicks by luring men in and then dumping them.

He didn't believe her story about the ex-boyfriend, though. With a frown, he crossed to his car. If she didn't tell anyone about the boyfriend, then how could he check it out? But that fact was also why he didn't believe it.

Caleb. Her brother would know, if no one else would. It was time he bought the guy a beer, did a little talking.

An hour later, after a few phone calls, he arrived at Lone Star, a steak place down the street from the hospital. But instead of heading into the restaurant, he grabbed a seat at the bar and watched for Caleb's arrival.

"Dr. Callaghan," Caleb McCallum said with a friendly smile. "Hope I haven't kept you waiting."

"Not at all, Caleb, and call me Hunter. What'll you have to drink?" Caleb had obviously seen his photo to identify him. But Hunter hadn't needed a photo. Caleb resembled his sister, only he didn't look soft, sweet, feminine.

"What you're having will do," Caleb said, nodding toward the draft beer Hunter had hardly touched. Hunter waved to the bartender. Then he debated his approach. Caleb took the lead however.

"R.J. said you had some questions about the security at the hospital. I'm a consultant for them, not actually in charge of security, but maybe I can answer your questions. What do you need to know?"

"No specific questions. More general things, like what's the crime in this area? Are there crimes in particular we need to be aware of? Have we had problems?''

The bartender delivered his beer, and Caleb took a sip before he answered. ''Maitland Maternity is in a safe neighborhood. However, in the past year, they've had a few problems. Mostly connected to the Maitlands themselves, rather than their patients.''

''Problems?''

Caleb grinned, ''Things like the day-care center being held hostage.''

Hunter had been looking for info about Bri. He'd never suspected there had been real problems. ''You're kidding.''

''Nope. But it was taken care of. Since the McCallum Wing opened, there hasn't been anything.''

''Is your sister going to put her babies in the day-care center?'' Hunter realized he'd been less than subtle when Caleb's eyes narrowed, eyes just like his sister's.

''Why do you want to know?''

Hunter drew a deep breath. He had a choice—continue to try to outfox this man, and Caleb appeared to be pretty sharp, or come clean. He looked at Caleb and made his decision. ''Because I think I'm the father of her babies.''

Caleb came off his stool, his hands forming tight fists.

''Wait a minute before you beat me to a pulp,'' Hunter asked, still calm. He wasn't surprised by Bri's

brother's response. He would've been disappointed if
he hadn't shown anger.

"Why would I wait?" Caleb growled.

"Because she says I'm not."

Caleb slowly sat back down. "Explain."

"It's a long story," Hunter warned. Caleb nodded,
and Hunter began his tale, starting seven months
ago....

"And you didn't know where to reach her?"

Hunter sighed. "I knew. But would you pursue a
woman who walked out on you after you thought
you'd found the one woman in the world perfect for
you?"

"So it was coincidence that you wound up here?"

"No. When word got out about the opening, I leapt
at the chance to come here. I'd told myself Bri was
a wealthy woman, playing games, not worth my time,
but when I got the opportunity, I took it."

"But you've left her here alone for seven months!"
Caleb exclaimed.

"Yeah, but I didn't know she was pregnant. I was
shocked when she walked into the office."

"And when you asked her about the babies?"

"She told me they weren't mine. That her old boyfriend met her at the airport and told her he was ready
to commit now. Then, six weeks later, when her pregnancy was discovered, he split." Hunter watched
Caleb closely.

"I don't remember any old boyfriend. I mean, there
was a man she was crazy about in college. Then she

overheard some gossip that he only wanted her money. She had me play a role in a little drama, pretending our dad's company had gone bankrupt, and we'd lost all our money. He started backing out of the relationship at once.''

"So she's had acting experience?"

"Not professionally," Caleb assured him with a grin.

"I didn't believe her story, but she was pretty good when she told it.''

"So what are you going to do?"

"What do you suggest?"

Caleb rubbed his chin, staring into space. "I don't know. She's stubborn.''

"Yeah. I think I'll try to be supportive, try to convince her I'm sincere, until after the babies are born. I don't want to put any stress on her now. Then, afterward, I'm going to insist on my parental rights.''

He stared at Caleb, his jaw firm. He wanted to know now if he was going to have a problem with her family.

"I don't blame you. But fight fair."

"I always do," he assured him.

"Will you offer marriage as an alternative?"

Hunter's immediate response was yes, but he didn't say it. He'd offered marriage already. She had two months of pregnancy left, if she went to full term. Maybe he should get to know her better. Then he could make his decision. "I'm not sure. I'll wait and see.''

Caleb seemed to be a reasonable man. "I understand. Shall I talk to my father, or my brother Adam?"

"No. I'll explain myself when the time comes. I'd appreciate you keeping what I've told you quiet."

"Okay. Just—just don't hurt her."

"No, but I won't give up my children."

FIRST THING the next morning, Hunter asked Helen to get the files on all the multiple birth patients from the various doctors on the staff. He wanted to review all the cases. "And in the future, Helen, tell the doctors I'll expect an update after each contact with the patient."

Helen nodded and excused herself.

Hunter hoped everyone else's reaction was as accepting as Helen's. But he wanted to be on top of the situation if they had difficulty with any patient. In particular, with Briana McCallum.

Helen returned a few minutes later and assured him all the doctors would send the files as soon as they could get them copied.

"Good. And after the files arrive, we'll need to schedule a visit with each doctor to go over the cases. Now, call Ms. McCallum and tell her I'm ready to go over some things with her as soon as she's free. And when she comes, I'd like you to bring in some milk and a muffin for her and coffee for me."

"Yes, sir."

He wanted to make sure she was eating properly.

He'd decided last night, lying in his bed, staring at the ceiling, that he wasn't going to risk his heart. But he was going to take care of his babies.

Only minutes later, Helen buzzed him to say Briana had arrived. He rose from his chair as the door opened and the mother of his daughters entered. Today she was wearing black slacks and a rose-colored top that matched her cheeks.

"Good morning," he said and gestured toward a large, comfortable chair in front of his desk. As she sat down, he found a low table near another chair, cleared everything off it and put it in front of Bri's chair. Then he lifted her feet to rest on the table.

"What—what are you doing?"

"It's better for pregnant women to keep their feet up."

"But I'm at work. I can't—"

"You're also one of our patients. Did you get a good night's sleep?" He didn't think so. She looked a little fragile this morning.

"Yes," she replied, her voice crisp. "I brought you a list of the problems we've dealt with in the past month. I've also set up a rotating checklist to stay on top of possible problems, and a contact sheet of people to call, depending on the specific problem. Other than me, of course. I'm supposed to be called when anything goes wrong."

"How very efficient of you. That will come in handy when you're on maternity leave. Have you thought about working half days now until you deliver?''

She glared at him. "No, I haven't!"

"Hmmm. Well, we'll talk about that later, after I review your file."

"After you what?"

He had been scanning the sheets of paper she'd given him. When he looked up in surprise, he discovered her leaning forward, stress on her features.

"I said, after I look at your file. I'm reviewing all the cases we're currently handling. I want to be familiar with all our patients before we have a surprise."

"I don't want you to look at my file!" She drew a deep breath, an obvious effort to calm down, but her gaze remained firmly on him. "I'm going to ask Abby to keep my file private."

"If she does, she'll have to operate at some other hospital," he said calmly.

She was sputtering, unable to get a coherent word out as Helen walked in carrying a tray.

"Ah, thanks, Helen. I think my guest is ready for a break."

Helen smiled back and then looked at Briana. "My dear, are you all right? Do I need to call Abby?" She shot Hunter a suspicious look, as if he were responsible for Bri's distress.

"Maybe you should ask Abby to visit with us as soon as she can, Helen. Bri and I are having a difference of opinion."

After another close look at Briana, Helen moved quickly to the door.

When it closed behind her, Bri found her voice. "You can't threaten to throw Abby out of her own family's hospital! You'll be out the door if you try such a thing!"

He smiled. "I won't have to threaten such a thing, Bri. Abby won't refuse to give me her files. It's my job to be on top of each situation. She knows that."

"No! You have nothing to do with my pregnancy. I told you that. I don't want strangers going through my file!"

"Stranger? You're calling me a stranger?"

"We're business acquaintances. It will be awkward to know that you've—you've read my files. And it's unnecessary. I'm perfectly healthy. Abby will tell you."

Hunter noted that her hands and lips were trembling. "Drink some milk and eat your muffin. It's good for the girls. Have you named them yet?" He'd thought about that last night.

"Yes."

"Well? Are their names secret, too?"

"No, of course not. I'm naming them Emily, Eleanor and Elizabeth. Emily was my mother's name."

"Elizabeth was *my* mother's name." He was amazed at how much that meant to him. He liked all three names, but Elizabeth was special to him.

"I didn't know that!"

He cocked one eyebrow. "I know."

Helen buzzed him again. "Abby is here."

Hunter stood again as Abby entered his office. "Good morning, doctor. Hope we didn't interrupt your busy schedule?"

"I don't start appointments until ten," Abby said with a smile, but her gaze was focused on Briana. "Hey, Bri, are you doing all right?"

"Fine," Bri said, but she didn't sound like it.

"Glad you're drinking milk. Mmm, that muffin looks good, too." Just as Abby finished, Helen came in with another coffee cup and saucer and poured her a cup of coffee from the pot already on the tray. "Oh, thank you, Helen."

Hunter slid the plate of muffins toward Abby. "Help yourself."

"Thanks. I missed breakfast this morning." She selected a muffin and bit into it, a look of pleasure on her face.

Hunter gave her a couple of minutes to enjoy the muffin. Then he cleared his throat. "Bri and I were having a difference of opinion and she was getting stressed. I thought it might smooth things out if you explained the necessity to her."

Abby looked first at Bri and then Hunter. "Of course, I'll try, though Bri's pretty savvy about things around here."

Bri wasn't looking at anyone, just staring into the glass of milk.

"I explained to her that I would be reviewing her

file, as I will all our patients. She would prefer that you keep her file to yourself.''

Abby stared at Bri. ''I can't do that, Bri. Dr. Callaghan is the head of obstetrics for the multiple birth wing. Of course he'll review the files. He's more experienced in multiple births than me.''

BRI KNEW when she'd lost a battle. And she also knew Dr. Hunter Callaghan's office was not the place to embark on her next battle. She'd talk privately to Abby about not having the man in the delivery room when it came time for her girls to arrive.

She carefully set the glass of milk, scarcely touched, back on the tray. ''I'm sorry. I should never have objected. It's just that I hadn't realized—he took me by surprise. Of course he'll need to review my file. But, as I told him, I'm in perfect health. I won't take up much of his time,'' she added with a smile at Abby. ''I'm sorry I interrupted your busy morning.'' She pushed herself up from the chair. ''Be sure to call if you need anything, Dr. Callaghan.''

''I need you to drink your milk.''

His calm words acted like a brick wall. An awkward silence filled the room. Drawing a deep breath, she said, ''Of course.'' Picking up the glass, she added, ''I'll take it with me and drink it while I'm working.''

''I'd rather you drink it here while you finish the muffin. I want to be sure that the girls get their nourishment.''

Bri shot a frantic look at Abby, but her doctor and friend nodded in agreement with him.

"I think Hunter's right, Bri. You look like you need to take a break."

Feeling trapped, Bri sank back into the chair and closed her eyes.

"I don't think she slept well last night," Hunter murmured to Abby, as if Bri suddenly couldn't hear.

"I'm still here," she said without opening her eyes. "I haven't left the building."

"Did you have a bad night?" Abby asked.

Bri licked her suddenly dry lips. "Yesterday was a little stressful."

Abby said, "I still think we should run some tests, put you in a hospital bed for a couple of days."

Bri's eyes popped open. "No, I'm fine!"

"Multiple-birth mothers frequently can't sleep well for long periods of time. Naps are necessary. That's why I suggested Bri start working half days. Then she could go home and take a nap," Hunter said.

"That's not a bad idea," Abby murmured.

Bri drew another deep breath to calm herself. "I appreciate your concern, and possibly I will do so before my delivery date, but I'd prefer to keep going as long as I can." She shot a pleading look at Abby.

"I think you can do so for a while longer without endangering the girls," Abby agreed.

"Good. Then I'll get back to work," Bri said and started to rise.

"The milk and muffin," Hunter reminded her, his blue eyes keeping her seated.

She struggled to hold on to her temper. "I'm not hungry!"

"I'll bet the girls are." He continued to stare at her, waiting for her to comply with his orders.

Finally, Bri grabbed the muffin and tore off a big bite, shoving it in her mouth. As soon as she'd chewed it, she took a long drink of milk. She repeated the process several more times until the muffin and milk had disappeared.

"Anything else, Dr. Callaghan?" she snapped, glaring at him.

"Not right this minute, Ms. McCallum. I'll let you know, probably around lunchtime." He smiled as if he were pleased with himself.

He might as well have waved a red flag in front of a bull. Bri felt her blood pressure rise, but she fought any response. "Then I'll return to my office. Thanks for stopping by, Abby." She hurried from the office before she lost the battle with her temper.

"I DON'T THINK there's a problem with Bri, except maybe her blood pressure," Abby said in a considering manner as she stared at Hunter.

He felt guilty. He knew he'd upset Bri and caused her blood pressure to go up. "You're right. I shouldn't have pressed her as much as I did, but I could tell she hadn't slept well last night. I was concerned."

"I'm sure Bri will appreciate that concern when she calms down. I'll check on her later today. If anything, she has too many people concerned about her. Even the mail boy checks on her when he delivers the mail. Everyone's kind of adopted her as our poster patient."

"Yes, I've noticed. I had no idea it would upset her so much for me to read her file. Good thing I didn't mention that I would observe her delivery." He was already determined to be there when his daughters entered the world. Emily, Eleanor and Elizabeth.

"You're right. I'm glad you didn't mention that. It might make it hard for Bri to face you after that." Abby stood, but she didn't start toward the door. Her gaze remained fixed on him.

Hunter stood also. "I appreciate your coming so quickly."

"No problem. Uh, did you and Bri know each other before you accepted the job?"

Hunter stood frozen, not sure what to say. He knew he didn't lie well, but how could he tell Abby the truth? It wouldn't take much to put together the time of the conference and seven months later.

"If I'd met Bri before, I can assure you I'd remember," he finally said. "She's a beautiful woman."

"True. She's special, too, warm and giving, which is why so many of us want her pregnancy to be a great success. She deserves happiness." With a nod and a smile, Abby left the office.

Hunter fell back into his chair, giving thanks that he'd found a way to answer Abby's question. Bri would be furious that he hadn't believed her story about her old boyfriend fathering the triplets. She'd definitely explode if she found out he'd shared his belief that the babies were his, with anyone.

Like everyone else in the building, he wanted Bri's pregnancy to have a happy ending. That's why he'd drop by her office about lunchtime to check on her.

Chapter Eight

"Bri, do you want me to bring you some lunch?" Lisa asked, interrupting Bri's concentration.

"No, thanks, Lisa. My dad is taking me to lunch."

"Okay, I'll switch the phones to voice mail until I get back."

Bri muttered "Okay" without looking up. She was trying to find a solution to the head nurse's rotation problem. It looked like it was going to cost more money and the budget was already tight.

Several minutes later, someone knocked on her open door. "Just a minute, Dad," she said, again not looking up.

"I didn't know we were that friendly, Bri. Besides, I'm older than you, but not all that much."

She looked up to find Hunter standing at her door.

"What are you doing here?" Not exactly a gracious response, but he made her nervous.

"Wondering what you were doing for lunch. Surely you weren't planning on skipping it?"

"No, my father—oh, hi, Dad," she said as her father appeared behind Hunter.

Hunter turned around and extended his hand. "Mr. McCallum, I was hoping to meet you soon. I'm Dr. Hunter Callaghan, the new head of obstetrics for the McCallum Wing. It's a fine facility."

"Dr. Callaghan! I'm glad to run into you. I apologize for missing the party yesterday, but I had an emergency come up at my company and couldn't get away."

Bri watched the two men uneasily. She didn't want her father getting too chummy with Hunter. "Are you ready, Dad? I can go now." The sooner the better.

"You're taking your daughter to lunch?" Hunter asked, an easy smile on his face. "I was just checking to see if she'd share lunch with me. I don't know too many people yet."

Bri froze. He managed to inject a lost-puppy tone in his voice, and she knew what was coming next.

"Well, feel free to join us. I'd love to have a chance to visit with you. You don't mind, do you, Bri?"

Oh, she minded. But it would make her father suspicious if she insulted her new boss.

"Um, why don't the two of you go ahead, and I'll take a rain check, Dad? I have a lot to do."

"No way," Hunter said. "I'm not going to ruin your lunch. I'll—I'll go down to the cafeteria."

She wanted to tell him to quit acting. But her father

immediately insisted they all three go, leaving her no choice.

"I've noticed Bri works too hard. I'm trying to talk her into working half days until the babies are born," Hunter said with a smile, as if he was only concerned with her health.

Of course, she couldn't think of another reason why he'd want her to work half days, but there had to be one.

"Not a bad idea. Come on, Briana. I'm hungry for a juicy steak," Jackson McCallum said, motioning for her to join them at the door.

"Hmm, I like your taste, Jackson. A steak sounds perfect. For Bri, too. She needs protein."

"We think alike, Hunter. I'm going to feel a lot better about Bri continuing to work knowing you're keeping an eye on her." Jackson beamed at the other man, and Bri ground her teeth.

"Dad! You know I can take care of myself!"

"I know, sweetheart. Come along now."

Jackson had a driver and a limo waiting downstairs to drive them the block and half to Lone Star. The hostess seated them in a circular booth, roomy for three, but Bri, seated between the two men, thought it was too small.

Once they'd ordered, Hunter began a flattering conversation about the wing Jackson had paid for, and the good it would do.

Jackson liked hearing all the praise. And it left Bri completely out of the conversation. She was glad about that. She was afraid her father might notice her antagonism if she was forced to converse with Hunter.

"And how do you feel about having triplet grand-daughters?" Hunter asked, suddenly claiming Bri's attention.

"Wonderful!" Jackson said, beaming at Hunter. "I didn't spend much time with my children when they were babies." He frowned. "I was too busy mourning their mother's death."

Hunter murmured a sympathetic phrase.

"But I'm going to take more time for these babies. Bri is going to name the firstborn after her mother. I'm pleased about that. And it's perfect timing. Adam is doing well with the company. We made all our money in oil well supplies. But times are changing. Adam is prepared. I'm not. So I'm retiring and play-ing with the girls."

"And she's naming one of the others after my mother," Hunter added.

Jackson stiffened. "Why?"

"It's purely accidental, Dad. When I chose the names, I didn't even know Hunter's mother's name."

Jackson stared at his daughter. "You didn't even know Hunter, I assume. Or is there something you're not telling me?"

Bri wanted to bury her face in her hands and curse Hunter Callaghan. But that would make her father even more suspicious. "Don't be silly, Dad. He just got here yesterday."

"He seems to have covered a lot of territory in two days," Jackson pointed out.

Hunter still seemed relaxed, unconcerned. "Of course I have. I asked for all the files on our multiple-birth patients at once so I could get up to speed. But I'll admit, I've given a little more attention to Bri than the others. That's because she's the favorite of the entire staff."

Jackson relaxed a little. "Yes, I've noticed that. They all check on her all the time."

"That's because she works too hard. They all know she pushes herself."

"I am still sitting here," she said sharply. "I'd appreciate it if you wouldn't talk about me as if I weren't."

"Sorry, sweetheart. Do you have children, Hunter?" Jackson asked.

Bri froze again. She wasn't sure Hunter had believed her lie. What would he answer?

With a laugh, as if he were telling a joke, Hunter said, "Not that I know of."

She slowly let out her breath. Hunter went on to explain that he hadn't found the woman he wanted to spend the rest of his life with.

Bri picked up her glass of water and sipped. After he'd made love to her, she'd thought for sure she had finally found the man of her dreams. Too bad he hadn't felt the same way.

"I guess Bri hasn't, either," Jackson said with a sigh. "We've tried to get her to tell us who the father is, but you've probably discovered she's pretty stubborn.''

"Dad!" she protested.

Jackson ignored her. "I have three children, and only one has married." He frowned. "And I hope that marriage holds together."

Bri reached over to take his hand as it rested on the table. "It will, Dad. Adam and Maggie will get past the problems."

"Sure. Of course, you're right. But it's ironic. My daughter-in-law wants a baby more than anything, and here Bri is, unmarried, but having three."

The waitress brought their steaks. Bri had such a nervous stomach, she didn't think she could take a single bite.

Jackson cut his steak and put a piece in his mouth. After chewing, he added, "Caleb, my third child, I don't think will ever marry. He keeps to himself."

"Dad, I'm sure Dr. Callaghan isn't interested in our family."

"Nonsense, Bri. I find it fascinating," Hunter assured her, a grin on his face.

"Then you should reciprocate. What kind of family do you have?" Bri hoped to irritate him, but he seemed pleased by her question.

"My mother passed away about three years ago. My dad is a retired doctor, my brother a corporate attorney. We all lived in Chicago until I moved."

"Did the move upset your father?" Jackson asked.

"Somewhat, but my brother is married with a couple of kids. Dad wants to stay close to his grandchildren. But he'll be coming to visit soon.''

''Let me know when he comes, Hunter, and we'll have a family dinner. Two old bachelors can compare notes.'' Jackson grinned, obviously looking forward to entertaining Hunter's father.

''Great. I'll do that. Dad would enjoy meeting—'' he paused and looked at Bri.

She froze again. He wouldn't! Surely he wouldn't!

''—some of the people I work with, and another bachelor with grandchildren.''

Bri slumped back against the booth.

''Sweetheart, you haven't eaten your steak. Don't forget the good doctor said you need the protein.''

Without looking at either man, she took a bite of potato. Then she cut a small piece of steak and valiantly chewed it. She only hoped the lunch would end soon, before she lost everything she managed to get down.

WHEN BRI GOT BACK to the office, she made a few quick decisions. Then she loaded up her briefcase with other problems to solve and moved to Lisa's desk. ''Lisa, I'm a little stressed today, so I'm taking half a day of vacation and I'm going home. If anything comes up that can't wait, call me at home. Otherwise I'll see you in the morning.''

''Can you drive yourself home?'' Lisa asked, standing, an anxious expression on her face.

"Lisa, I'm going home to put my feet up. Don't worry about me."

"Should I call Dr. Abby or Dr. Callaghan?"

"No!" Bri took a deep breath. "Just let me take the afternoon off without any complications, Lisa. That's all I want."

She hurried out of the office to get away from any more questions or suggestions. She appreciated everyone's concern for her and her babies, but sometimes she wished she'd moved to a town where no one knew her.

Half an hour later, she was feeling much better. As soon as she got home, she'd stripped and filled the tub with warm water and bubble bath. She stretched out in the oversized tub and breathed deeply, trying to forget about the stressful lunch. It had lasted forever because neither man would leave until she'd finished every bite of her steak and potato.

She wanted to murder Hunter Callaghan. He'd known what he was doing with each teasing response. He'd even known she was upset. What a jerk!

"You should've known better. That was what you thought he was seven months ago. People don't change."

She shook her head. "And now I'm talking to myself. What am I going to do?"

She slid a little lower into the water, trying to clear her mind. She didn't want to think about a future with Hunter Callaghan around.

The phone rang. She considered getting out of the

tub, but with her bulky shape right now, she'd never get to the phone in time to answer it. Besides, she had her answering machine on.

She could vaguely hear a man's voice, but not loud enough to recognize it. She'd check the message when she got out.

Ten minutes later, when her skin felt as though it was shriveling, she began the laborious task of getting out of the tub. Once she was upright, she wrapped her body in a big bath towel, thinking she looked like a house moving down the road. All she lacked was a tow truck.

The doorbell rang, and she frowned. No one should expect her to be home, so who could it be? She decided not to answer it and continued down the hall to her bedroom.

But she stopped because the caller abandoned the doorbell and began beating on the door itself, yelling her name. Afraid a neighbor might call the police, she rushed to the door. "Who is it?"

"Bri? Open the door!"

Recognizing the caller as Dr. Hunter Callaghan, Bri wasn't inclined to follow his order. "What's wrong?"

"I want to make sure you're all right!"

"I'm fine. Go away!"

"I'm calling an ambulance and the police if you don't open the door in one minute."

"Why?"

"I have to check your blood pressure!" Then he began pounding the door again.

With a sigh, she opened the door. "Stop that! You're going to upset my neighbors!"

Hunter stared at her, reminding her she was wrapped in a bath towel. She began shoving the door closed, but he stuck his foot in it.

"I'm coming in, Bri. I want to check your blood pressure," Hunter insisted.

"Fine! I have to go get dressed." She gave up the battle with the door and stomped out of her living room. She came back a few minutes later, wearing a muumuu she'd bought in Hawaii several years ago. It was the easiest thing to wear when she was relaxing.

Hunter was pacing the room, checking his watch every few seconds.

"Don't let me keep you if you've got an appointment," she said, her chin in the air.

He immediately opened his medical bag. "Sit down. I want to check your blood pressure. I noticed you were stressed at lunch."

"Of course I was stressed!" Bri yelled at him. "You were upsetting me on purpose."

"What?" Hunter responded, shock on his face. "I did not do that! I was visiting with your father, that's all."

She still stood, staring at him, when he reached out. "You're weaving. Sit down before you fall down."

She sank into the nearest chair and leaned back. "Look, just go back to the hospital and leave me alone. I'll be fine if I get some time alone."

Her phone rang again.

She stared at it, amazed that she was getting all these calls when she should've been at work.

Without asking permission, Hunter snatched up the receiver. "She's okay, Lisa. I don't know—why didn't you answer the phone?" he asked Bri.

"Because I was taking a bubble bath to relax— until someone began pounding on my door."

He only repeated the first part of her sentence. "Yeah, I'll stay with her a little while until I'm sure she's okay. Yeah." He hung up the phone.

"Don't mind me," she muttered.

"Sorry, I should've asked permission, but I was sure it was Lisa. When I called and couldn't get an answer, we both panicked."

She closed her eyes. "I didn't think you knew where I lived," she muttered.

"Lisa gave me directions."

She opened her eyes when he put the blood pressure cuff on her arm.

"Just lie back and relax," he said softly.

The problem was she knew her blood pressure was high. She didn't want him to order her to the hospital.

When he released the pressure and took the cuff off without saying a word, she prompted him. "Well?"

"It's a little high, but I know you don't want to go to the hospital. I'll agree to that if you'll let me treat you here."

"What kind of treatment?"

"Remember when I told you I gave great foot massages?"

"Yes." He couldn't mean what he was implying.

"I'm going to give you a foot massage."

"Don't be ridiculous. I'm fine."

"Stay calm. It won't hurt."

"I don't want you touching me." She was afraid it would remind her too much of making love with the man.

"Bri, either you let me rub your feet and calm you down, or you *will* have to go to the hospital."

"No, I— Okay. A foot massage," she rapidly agreed. Even if she protested going to the hospital, it would only take one call to Abby or her father for Dr. Callaghan to make it impossible for her to stay home.

"Let's go to your bedroom."

"No! I can sit on the couch."

"We'll be more comfortable on the bed. Do you have any foot cream?"

"Yes. It's in the bathroom. It's pink, scented peppermint. I'll—"

"Go on to your bedroom and pile up lots of pillows behind you. I'll get the cream."

He entered the room only a couple of minutes later while she was still piling up pillows on the bed.

"I found the cream and a towel. Now, do you have a book to read, something you enjoy?"

She nodded. "I—I started a book last night, but I fell asleep."

"Get it while I pour you a glass of milk."

"But I just ate!"

He ignored her and headed for the kitchen.

"Fine. Bring me milk. If it will get rid of you, I'll even drink it!" she muttered. Then she grabbed her book, turned on the bedside lamp and crawled up in the middle of the bed.

Hunter put a glass of milk beside her on the lamp table. "I'll have to turn my back to you to do a good job, so just relax and read, drink a little milk."

Somehow, having his back to her made everything easier. He pulled her muumuu up to her knees, but no higher. Then he poured cream into his hands, holding it there for it to warm. He took her right foot into his large, warm palms and began to rub in the cream. His strong fingers kneaded the sole of her foot and she sighed.

"I'm not hurting you, am I?" he asked.

"No. No, it feels—good." She hated to admit it, but it did feel great. She hadn't seen her feet often in the last couple of months. Though she wore sensible shoes, as her weight increased, her feet grew more stressed.

Her left foot edged toward her right one, as if making its own plea not to be ignored.

Half an hour later, Bri lay back against the pillows, the milk glass empty and her eyes closed. She hadn't read a single page of the romance novel. She'd been too busy indulging in her own fantasy.

WHEN HUNTER finally felt he'd done all he could, he peeped over his shoulder to discover a relaxed Bri, her eyes closed, breathing deeply. He rose from the bed and moved around to the side, putting his fingers on her pulse.

She was doing much better. When he called her name, she didn't respond, and he realized she'd gone to sleep.

Excellent. He'd felt so guilty when he'd reached her office, and Lisa had said she'd gone home because of stress. He hadn't intentionally teased her about the babies being his. Well, maybe a little. But he hadn't realized how fragile she was.

And they *were* his babies. He felt sure of that now. Otherwise, why would she be so worried about him talking to her father? She'd denied his fatherhood and lied about an ex-boyfriend. That wasn't fair.

But he couldn't put any pressure on her. Just hinting that she might have lied could've brought on early labor. He was going to have to be very careful until she went into labor.

No offer of marriage.

No claim of fatherhood.

No seducing her.

It was amazing that he still found her sexy when she was seven months pregnant with triplets. But he did. He'd like to kiss her, just to be sure the magic was still there, but he felt sure that would bring on more stress.

He wanted to cup her cheek as she lay sleeping, but he couldn't even do that.

With a sigh, he pulled the cover over her so she wouldn't get chilled. Then he left the bedroom. Picking up the phone, he called Lisa. "She's gone to sleep. I need to know the best place to order her a decent dinner. Someone who delivers."

"Well, mostly fast food does the deliveries. I could get her some supper from Austin Eats and take it by there after work, if you'd like."

"That would be great, Lisa. I'm on my way back to the office. I'll stop by and give you some money."

"Oh, that's okay, I'll—"

"I'll be there in a minute."

Now he'd know she would eat a good dinner and then go back to sleep. And while he knew she had plenty of money to pay for her meals, it pleased him to pay for it himself. After all, she was the mother of his children—whether she admitted it or not.

Chapter Nine

Bri was feeling better than she had in days when she reached the office the next morning—except for the guilt she felt about the mean things she'd thought about Hunter.

Because he'd been wonderful.

Knowing she didn't want to go to the hospital, he'd spent a lot of time calming her down—with a foot rub. He'd actually put her to sleep. Then he'd made sure she hadn't had to cook a meal. Lisa had arrived with a nutritious meal, including milk, from Austin Eats.

She'd immediately explained that Dr. Callaghan had insisted on giving money for dinner for both of them. "He was so sweet, Bri, so concerned for you. I know he's a doctor, but he's only known you a couple of days."

Bri had agreed that Dr. Hunter Callaghan was very sweet, outstandingly so. Which irritated her. Which made her angry again. Which made her think bad thoughts about Dr. Hunter Callaghan!

She knew she'd have to thank him this morning for his consideration. And that thought made her blood pressure rise again.

"Okay, has my schedule changed this morning?" she asked, hoping to discuss business rather than the sainthood of Dr. Callaghan.

"Oh, yes. Dr. Callaghan's having a department heads' meeting at nine o'clock and wants you to attend." Lisa pulled out Bri's calendar and showed her how she'd cleared her schedule by moving several appointments to the afternoon. "But if you want to go home at noon, I can transfer the appointments to tomorrow morning."

Bri suspected the idea of her going home at noon came from Hunter, which irritated her. She'd remembered how he'd said his mother stayed home with her children. How he hoped to give his children the same kind of home life.

That, of course, was before she'd realized she was going to be carrying his children. She'd spent her entire life preparing for this job as hospital administrator. She'd wanted to contribute in some way, to others, so they wouldn't die as her mother had. And she was good at it. She should give that up? Abandon her life's dream? She could provide for her children and love them. She knew about the love children needed. Besides, these were her babies, not Hunter's. He had nothing to say about it.

"Do you need anything else, Bri?"

"No, Lisa, thank you. You've taken care of everything.'' And obviously followed Hunter's lead. She liked Lisa, and she was a good worker. Bri hoped she didn't have to have her transferred.

She went to her desk and removed her shoes. She kept a stool under the desk to rest her feet on. She certainly wasn't going to a meeting in Hunter's office with her feet all swollen.

She arrived at Hunter's office at exactly nine o'clock. Helen waved her through to his office. She hadn't wanted to be late, but she also hadn't wanted to arrive before anyone else got there.

When she opened the door, it appeared she was the last to enter. All the department heads were gathered around Hunter's desk. Some were seated in folding chairs, clearly brought in for the meeting. The unusual thing was the leather wing chair she'd occupied before, the most comfortable chair in the room except for Hunter's, was empty.

Joanna, the head of the cafeteria, leapt to her feet and gestured to the big chair. ''Dr. Callaghan reserved this chair for you, Bri, so you'd be comfortable,'' she announced with a smile. Though she first smiled at Bri, Bri noticed how it slid to Hunter's face, filled with admiration for him.

''How kind of him. But totally unnecessary. Does someone else want the honor?''

No one would take the chair, of course. Not when Dr. Callaghan had designated it for her.

She felt like an ungrateful jerk, but she wanted to

walk out on the meeting. She hated being the center of attention. She had no choice, so she sat down.

Hunter immediately stood, as did Joanna. He said, "I asked Joanna to provide us with a few snacks. A reward for the good work you people have been doing."

While Joanna uncovered trays on the big coffee table before the sofa, Hunter leaned down and pulled out a padded footstool for Bri. She stared at it, sure it hadn't been in his office before.

"Where did that come from?" she whispered fiercely.

"It's a gift from one of our donors. I thought it would come in handy for you." He smiled after putting her feet on the stool, but he kept his eye on her, as if he thought she might kick him while he was squatting in front of her.

Not a bad idea.

Joanna came over, carrying a small tray holding a glass of milk and several pieces of banana nut bread. "Sam baked the banana nut bread special for you, Bri, 'cause he knew you'd be here this morning."

Bri pasted on a smile. "Tell Sam thank you for me."

"Here, Joanna, put it on the corner of my desk. I think Bri can reach everything from there," Hunter suggested.

Oh, yes, she could reach it, but it would be in plain sight of everyone, so they could monitor her appreciation of Sam's special treat. She glared at Hunter, but he ignored her response.

"Well now, first of all, I want to congratulate you on the state of our wing. I've never seen a special unit function as well as this one does. It's a pleasure to come to work here each morning."

Bri knew she was being difficult. No one could find anything wrong with Hunter's opening. But she did! Butter wouldn't melt in his mouth. When was the other shoe going to drop? And if he talked long enough, she'd think up some more appropriate clichés!

But no matter how long she listened, he said nothing she could hold against him. Except for preparing her team for when she was on maternity leave, however, he made it clear he expected her to return to her job.

Liar! She knew that wasn't what he wanted.

Of course, he did pause occasionally to remind her to eat the special bread Sam made for her. And to drink her milk for the babies' sake.

Then he stopped talking and asked them to tell him what they needed and what problems they were having.

It was a management technique Bri had used, but she hadn't expected such consideration from Hunter. He didn't hurry the staff, and never denounced their ideas. Occasionally, he complimented some suggestions but explained that they had limited funds.

She'd expected her team to ask for everything possible, thinking Bri could strong-arm the money out of her father's pocket. Hunter pointed out the generosity of their benefactor, her father, and the need to stay within budget unless what was needed would save lives.

And dammit! They listened to him.

When he dismissed her team, Bri could read the satisfaction in their faces. She began the struggle to rise.

"Stay seated, Bri. I have a couple of other things to go over," he added softly before he escorted the others out. Everyone turned and stared at her, smiles on all their faces.

As if they thought Hunter was flirting with her!

That realization sent her blood pressure over the roof. How idiotic! They were both professionals. How could her people think that she was interested in romance at a time like this?

It was Hunter's fault! He was paying her too much attention because he thought her babies were his, too. Well, she'd set him straight about that. Right now!

He closed the door and walked back toward her.

"These are not your babies!" she snarled as he got closer.

"Why are you bringing that issue up now?" he asked calmly.

"Did you see their faces? They think we're—we're interested in each other! You've got to stop paying me special attention!"

"But I *am* interested in you, Bri," he said, his gaze fixed on her. Those damned blue eyes.

"Only because you think these babies have something to do with you. And they don't!"

He sat in the chair next to her, the one earlier occupied by Joanna, and reached for her wrist. "I think you're getting upset again. You've got to stop that, or I'll have to put you in the hospital. It's bad for the girls."

She closed her eyes and leaned her head against the back of the chair. "It's your fault."

"I know. I warned you I gave good foot massages, but I didn't expect you to beg for another one so soon," he said, a grin on his handsome face.

She groaned. Then she sat up. Before she could start to rise, however, he reached for her feet. "I don't have any lotion here, but I can do a quick massage while we talk."

"No! No, you can't. What if—" Then she groaned again as his magic fingers pressed into her flesh.

And Helen entered the office.

Bri tried to jerk her feet out of his hands, but he held on. "Yes, Helen?"

"I have all the doctors' files for you to review, Hunter. Oh, Bri, you lucky girl. When I was pregnant, I would've done anything for a foot rub. My husband refused to give me one." She sighed. "Is there anything else, Hunter?"

"No, Helen, thank you." And he continued to massage Bri's feet.

Bri covered her face with her hands. "Hunter, please stop. The entire hospital is going to be talking about us if you don't." She realized her voice had descended to the level of pleading, but she didn't know how else to get him to stop.

"Honey, I'm just trying to make things easier for you, that's all. I'll explain it to anyone who says differently. Indirectly, you're my patient. I know what's good for pregnant ladies."

"I—I have to go. I have a job to do. It's very important that I do my job."

"I know. Have you arranged for some help after the babies are born?"

"Grace says she knows of someone," she muttered.

"Grace? Oh, I remember. The lady who took care of you and your brothers. She can't come?"

"She's too old to take on three babies. And I'll need help with the cooking and housecleaning. I've even been thinking about hiring someone now. I don't have a big place, but it can get dirty fast. And sometimes I don't feel up to doing laundry and the dishes."

She hadn't meant to tell him that, but it seemed once she started talking about it, she couldn't stop. She didn't want to complain at the hospital. And she couldn't talk to her father about such things. He'd move an army into her house and she'd lose her privacy.

"Why don't you call Grace today and talk to her about it? And be sure it's someone who can cook.

You shouldn't have to cook dinner after working all day.''

"Oh," she said with a big sigh. "That would be heavenly, wouldn't it?''

"Yeah. Will you call Grace?''

"I shouldn't. I can manage until the girls get here. I'll just get lazy if I don't keep moving.''

His blue eyes darkened, but his face remained calm. Suddenly he leaned forward and kissed her— on the lips. It happened again. Even though the kiss was almost brotherly, her response wasn't. The magic she'd felt the first time was mild compared to what she felt today with just the touch of his lips. Had she lost her mind? She wanted more and almost reached out for him. Fortunately, his phone rang before she could actually make such a disastrous mistake.

"Go back to your office, honey. I'll check on you later.''

"Yes, uh, but you shouldn't call me honey. We're professionals," she reminded him as she closed the door behind her.

At least she hoped she was.

DR. ZACH BEAUMOUNT was on the phone Helen told him. Hunter had met the obstetrician and liked him. He reached for the stack of files, finding the ones belonging to Beaumont as Helen put the call through.

"Zach? Hunter here. How can I help you?''

"Did you get my files?''

"Just got them. I haven't had a chance to go over them yet. Is there a problem?"

"Not with those cases. But I saw a new patient today."

Hunter waited for him to come to the point. Multiple births could show themselves very early.

"She's about five and a half months pregnant...and carrying four babies, two sets of identical twins."

"What's her history?"

"I'm the first doctor she's seen."

"Damn! Any problems?"

"The babies are undersized. I made sure she got a supply of vitamin tablets. I don't think she has any money. I want to put her on our charity list."

"Of course. Do you have an address or phone number?"

"She's staying at a boardinghouse. Says she's a widow, but she's only seventeen. Her landlady convinced her to come see me."

"Okay, I'll authorize putting her on the charity list and I'll send our social worker to visit with her and take information. Do you think she'll be able to carry them long?"

"I doubt it. She's small. I don't think she's eating well. I'd like to put her in the hospital as soon as I can talk her into it."

"That's probably a good idea. We'll get the ball moving from this end. Thanks for letting me know, and send a copy of her file to Helen."

"Right away. Thanks for supporting me on this case."

Hunter smiled. "That's what I'm here for."

He knew everyone would want to test him out, to see how cooperative he'd be. They'd soon learn that babies' lives were his first priority. If he had to go out and solicit funds himself, he didn't want any multiple birth to occur in less than exemplary conditions so that the children had the best chance of survival.

He rang for Helen, and she hurried in, a steno pad in her hand. He immediately gave her orders. Her concern for the young woman, even though she didn't know her, came through loud and clear. Hunter was pleased.

"Let me know when the file gets here and when everything has been taken care of."

"Yes, doctor, at once."

As she got up to go to her desk, he stopped her. "Do you happen to have Caleb McCallum's work number? Or could you get it for me?"

"Of course. Is there a problem with security?"

"I just have a question for him," Hunter assured her. He wasn't about to tell her that he was going to interfere with Briana's personal life. But he was.

Within minutes, he got Caleb on the line.

"Hey, doc, what's up?"

"Caleb, I need Grace's phone number."

"Grace?" he repeated, as if he'd never heard the name before.

"Yeah, you know, the lady who took care of you when you were little."

"Yeah, I know, but how do you know? And what do you want her number for? She's retired."

Caleb, it appeared, didn't take anyone on trust right away. With a sigh, Hunter said, "Grace is going to recommend someone to take care of Bri and the babies. Bri is determined to make it on her own until the babies are born, but I think she needs help now. Someone to cook and clean, to make sure she eats properly."

"Oh. Did you discuss it with Bri?"

"Yes, I did, but she's stubborn. She admitted it sounded wonderful to have some help, but she's afraid everyone will think she's lazy, which is ridiculous."

"Yeah, it is. Okay, here's Grace's number, but you do realize Bri is going to be furious that you're interfering, don't you?"

"Yeah, but I'm going to try to get Grace on my side. So keep our conversation to yourself."

"You got it, doc."

Hunter wrote down the number.

When he dialed the number, a sweet feminine voice answered.

"Is this Grace?"

"Yes. Who's speaking?"

"You don't know me. I'm the new obstetrics head at the McCallum Wing."

"Dr. Callaghan? Of course I know who you are. Is

there a problem with my volunteering? I do love it so. I hope I'm—"

"I didn't know you volunteered."

"I usually volunteer in the preemie nursery in Maitland, but when you get babies in your nursery, I'm transferring over there. I'm coming in today for a tour."

"You are? What time?"

"My tour is at one."

"Come at eleven and I'll explain why I need your help. Then we'll both go take Bri to lunch. Is it a deal?"

"It's a deal. I'm very interested. Everything's okay, isn't it? I mean the babies and all?"

"I'm trying to make sure of that. But you know how stubborn Briana is."

"Oh, yes. I'll be there at eleven."

Then he buzzed Helen. "I want you to call Bri and tell her that I expect her to join me for lunch today. I have a special guest I want her to entertain. And don't take no for an answer. Tell her we'll drop by her office at noon to pick her up. We'll eat in the cafeteria."

"What if she refuses?" Helen asked, frowning.

"It's your job to make sure she doesn't, Helen."

She stared at him. "I don't want to upset her."

"Helen, Briana's former nanny is coming to lunch today. She's going to volunteer in the nursery as soon as we have some customers. Her presence is a surprise for Bri, so keep it a secret, but it's a surprise Bri will enjoy.''

After Helen withdrew, Hunter sighed. His secretary thought he was a bully. That was a fine state of affairs. And he was trying to be so tactful.

Right on time, Grace arrived at his office. She was elderly, he'd guess in her seventies, but she looked healthy and had the most serene expression on her face he'd ever seen.

''Dr. Callaghan, I'm anxious to hear what you want to discuss with me.''

''Bri mentioned that you were going to recommend someone to help her with the babies.''

''Why, yes, a very nice, experienced woman.''

''Is the woman prepared to do housecleaning and cooking, also?''

''Of course,'' Grace replied, a puzzled look on her face.

''Well, I'd like Briana to go ahead and hire the woman now. She goes home exhausted. I'm worried she's not eating properly because she's too tired to cook. She admitted she's too tired to do housecleaning, and she worries that if she hires someone now, everyone will think she's lazy.''

''That's ridiculous! The poor child is carrying three babies. After what happened to her mother, I worry about her all the time.''

''Could you convince her she should go ahead and hire the woman so they can get to know each other before the babies come? Tell her she'll be happier if she knows who's taking care of her babies from the word go?''

''That's a very good idea, Dr. Callaghan,'' Grace assured him with a smile. ''Of course I can do that.''

''Good,'' he said, smiling.

''And with you recommending it, I don't see how she can resist.''

''No! Don't mention me!''

Chapter Ten

Bri sat hunched over her desk, irritation coursing through her. A special guest! Hunter needed her to entertain the person! Right! All he was doing was supervising her eating habits. Dr. Hunter Callaghan was an interfering, bossy man. How were they going to stop the gossip if he didn't stop this silliness?

It was almost twelve. Helen had made it clear in her phone call that the invitation wasn't one Briana could refuse. So, where was the big man? He seemed to think he could order her life around. The least he could do was be on time!

Just as the hands on her watch reached straight-up twelve, a soft knock sounded on her door. She called, "Come in," ready to be difficult.

The door opened and Grace, her darling Grace, appeared. Bri struggled to her feet and went to the door to wrap her arms around her true mother. "Grace! What are you doing here? Is everything all right? Oh, I have to go to lunch with someone, or I'd take you—"

"Calm down, child. You're going to lunch with me. Hunter arranged it all. Isn't he a darling man?"

Bri tried to stifle her groan. Another person singing his praises? She didn't think she could stand it. "Yes, fabulous," she said, trying to dredge up enthusiasm. "Why are you here?"

"I'm taking a tour of the nursery. Once you start having babies there, I'm going to volunteer. I've had experience with multiple-birth babies, you know," she added with a beaming smile.

Bri hugged her again. "I know you have. And you're a terrific mother substitute."

"Bless you, child," Grace responded, tears in her eyes. Then she stepped back from Bri. "Now, how are you managing? Let me look at you. My, you've gotten quite a bit bigger since the last time I saw you."

"Yes," Bri agreed with a sigh.

"That's good, child. You want these babies to grow so when they're born, they'll be okay."

"Of course," Bri agreed, smiling.

Grace frowned. "But you also need to take care of yourself. How are you managing?"

"You two ladies ready for lunch?" Hunter called. He'd stopped at Lisa's desk and talked to her. Now he stepped to the door of Bri's office.

Bri stared at him. "Yes, of course, but we don't want to take up your valuable time. I'll take care of Grace."

"Oh, no, you don't. Grace is my date. I'm just

being nice, letting you come along. Let's go. We don't want to be at the back of the cafeteria line. They've got chocolate pie today.''

Grace took her hand and pulled her toward Hunter. Before Bri knew it, they were in the elevator. She was going to share lunch again with Hunter. With another family member. Grace might not be a blood relative, but she certainly was part of Bri's family.

It seemed to Bri that everyone in the cafeteria was staring at them as they went through the line. Hunter and Grace kept up a rambling conversation about their food selections. Grace added several vegetables to Bri's tray. When Hunter added the chocolate pie, Bri finally protested, but he ignored her. He was too busy waving to the cashier to charge all three meals to his account.

Oh, good, that wouldn't cause any talk!

''Hunter,'' she whispered. ''Let me pay for me and Grace. It will cause less talk.''

''Honey, you've got to quit worrying about gossip. It's not important.'' Then he raised his voice. ''Pick wherever you want to sit, Grace. We'll follow.''

Grace selected a table for four right in the middle of the room where everyone would see them.

Bri took a seat next to Grace, hoping Hunter would sit down on the older woman's other side, which would give her a little breathing room. She should've known better. He, of course, sat down next to her.

''How did you know Grace was coming today?'' Bri suddenly asked.

"She knows Helen and called to ask her to lunch. When Helen told me who she was, I included the two of us."

Bri turned and looked at Grace. "I didn't know you knew Helen that well. Weren't you going to at least come see *me?*"

"Of course I was. But I knew how busy you'd been with the opening; I didn't want to cause you any stress. But I'm glad I did see you. Without what we added to your tray, you wouldn't have had much to eat. Aren't you taking care of yourself and the girls?"

"Sure I am. But I already had a snack today. Lately it seems I'm eating constantly." She slanted a glare toward Hunter. "And where is Helen?"

Hunter's face grew serious. "Zach Beaumont got a new patient today. We're anxious to get her in the hospital and Helen volunteered to stay at work to speed everything up." He smiled at her before taking a bite of meat loaf. "But you're coming along nicely. I looked at the latest ultrasound this morning. The girls are a nice size. But I do worry about you not getting enough rest."

Grace immediately picked up that point. "Are you trying to do too much, darling?"

"Of course not!" Bri protested. "My place is even a little messy, because I'm really not doing too much. Really, Grace, I'm doing fine."

"Well, I was thinking it might be a good idea for Alice to start working for you *before* the babies come. Then you'll feel more comfortable, turning the children over to her while you get some rest. And it wouldn't hurt for her to cook and clean a little now.''

Bri carefully put down her silverware and turned to Hunter. ''You need to keep your nose out of my business!''

He tried to look innocent, but she had no doubt that he had put Grace up to this sudden idea. She started to rise and he clamped his hand on her arm, keeping her seated.

''Really, Bri, I'm sure I taught you better manners than that. The man is just trying to take care of you,'' Grace insisted, frowning. ''I'm thankful he contacted me. I had no idea you were ready for help. Why hadn't you called me? I could at least come by every other day or so and do some laundry or something.''

''Grace, I wouldn't ask that of you!''

''Well, thankfully, it's not necessary. I talked to Alice this morning. We thought it would be good if she came in for half a day. She could do laundry, change the bed linens, things like that, in the afternoon and then have dinner ready for you when you got home.''

''That sounds lovely, but it's totally unnecessary, Grace. I can take care of myself,'' Bri assured her.

''Of course you can, but this would be for the girls. They need their rest so they can grow. Please do this for me, darling Bri, so I won't have to worry about you so much.''

Hunter sat back and watched Grace at work. She'd outflanked Bri at every turn. He could use her on his staff. Most important of all, she was getting Bri to do the right thing.

"In fact," Grace added, "it will be good for Alice, too. She's a widow, you know, and she spends too much time alone. She'll get to know your kitchen and how you like things done, instead of having to learn all that with the complication of three babies."

Hunter grinned. Now she was telling Bri she was being selfish not giving Alice a job at once. When Bri turned to glare at him, as if she'd been able to read his thoughts, he wiped away the grin. "That's good thinking, Grace."

"Of course you would think so. Where did you get Grace's number? I didn't tell you her last name," Bri said.

"I never reveal my sources," he said with a smile.

"Darling Bri, you should've let me know you were struggling," Grace said, patting her hand. "And I should've checked on you more often. I'm afraid I'm spoiling Douglas, centering my world around him. Tsk!"

"Grace, you've always spoiled all of us. That's why we love you so much," Bri said with a gentle smile. "Tell Alice I'd love for her to start part-time to get adjusted. I'd appreciate her help."

"Wonderful, dear. I'll give her my key to your place and I'm sure she'll come in about one today. She promised she'd cook a healthy meal for you."

"I don't know if I have anything there to cook."

Bri frantically tried to go through her pantry in her head.

"I knew it. You've been neglecting yourself."

'It's just so hard to carry in groceries right now, Grace," Bri protested.

"Alice will do whatever grocery shopping is necessary. She'll save the receipt and you can reimburse her." Grace turned to Hunter. "I'm so glad you called me, Hunter. Bri will be feeling much better with the proper care."

Though Bri glared at him again, Hunter felt like celebrating. He'd succeeded, thanks to Grace. "Eat your pie, Bri," was his only comment, however.

"Aren't you worried about the calories I'm consuming? I'm surprised you don't have a calculator out counting each one!" she exclaimed.

"If anything, you're too thin. I want a little baby fat on the girls when they're born," he assured her.

"You should see my Bri when she's not pregnant," Grace said. "She's a beautiful woman!"

Hunter smiled at Bri. "Yes, I'm sure she is." He could remember her in that storeroom, wrapped around his body, her scent filling his nostrils, her warmth heating up his own.

"Are you married?" Grace asked, looking from him to Bri and back again.

"Grace!" Bri protested.

"No, I'm not. Want to do some matchmaking? I'm not against it," he said, his smile widening, knowing it would infuriate Bri.

"Well, it's a thought. But I suppose we should wait until after the girls are born. You're not one of those men who only like boy babies, are you?"

"Not at all. Three identical little girls, looking like their mama, couldn't make a more beautiful picture."

"Exactly!" Grace replied, almost clapping her hands in approval. "I'll bring some baby pictures of Bri and her brothers the next time I come."

"I'll look forward to it," he assured her, seeing the babies in his mind's eye. Maybe they'd have blue eyes like his. But Bri's hazel eyes were so beautiful.

Grace interrupted his thoughts. "The main thing is to get them here safely."

"You're so right," he agreed. "That's my number-one concern, too."

"I'm still here," Bri reminded them. "You've rearranged my life. The least you can do is talk to me as though I'm a real person."

"Being pregnant makes her a little testy. She normally has a wonderful personality," Grace assured him.

"I feel like an old maid someone is trying to auction off. Please, Grace, I'm fine. I don't need a husband."

April Sullivan stopped by their table, holding her full tray. "You looking for a husband, Bri?" she asked, obviously having overheard Bri's last words.

"No! But some of my family seem to think I can't manage alone," Bri told her friend, disgust in her voice. "Have you met Grace? She and her husband took care of my brothers and I when we were babies. She's going to be volunteering in the nursery as soon as we get babies," she added.

"Then I hope you're ready soon. We've got twins that I think will arrive within the week."

"Excellent!" Grace said, beaming. "I love babies."

"Well, you must be good if you took care of Bri and her brothers," April said with a smile.

"We'd ask you to join us," Hunter said, "but I think we're finished. I know I have to get back so I can review the files. What's the name of the patient soon to deliver?"

April gave him the woman's name. He pulled out a piece of paper from his pocket and scribbled down the last name. "Ready, ladies?"

"You go ahead. Grace and I want to visit with April for a while, if you don't mind."

"Not at all," he agreed. He stood and held out the chair for April to sit down. "I enjoyed the company, ladies. And, Grace, thanks for your help." He bent over and kissed the older woman's cheek. Then he did the same to Bri. "Didn't want to leave you out, honey. See you later."

"NOT IF I see you first," Bri muttered, horrified that he'd kissed her cheek in front of half the hospital. When she dared look at April, she found her friend staring. "That meant nothing," she hurriedly said.

"He is such a sweet boy, isn't he, Bri?" Grace said, still smiling.

Bri couldn't think of what to say.

"Everyone likes him," April offered. "I've only heard praise since he got here." But she still kept her gaze on Bri, as if she expected Bri to make a major announcement at any moment.

"April, don't pay any attention to anything he does. He's intent on teasing me."

"But he just met you," April pointed out, a puzzled look on her face.

Bri felt she had to come up with something, some reason for his familiarity, or everyone was going to be convinced she and Dr. Callaghan had something going. Which was utterly ridiculous. "Uh, I met him once at a conference."

"Really? Did you keep in touch?"

"Not exactly. We have mutual acquaintances. It's nothing." Definitely nothing. She hoped if she downplayed it, no one would try to figure out which conference. She'd gone to three different ones before the wing opened.

"Oh, I guess that explains it. But you might keep him in mind for, you know, later on, after the girls are born."

"Exactly what I say," Grace agreed enthusiastically.

"I can't believe the two of you. Look at me! Do I look like I'd be thinking anything about romance? I'm like a beached whale at this point. And I don't feel friendly toward the sex that got me this way!''

April grinned. ''That will pass. I know you love your girls already.''

''Yes, and I'm concentrating on them and no one else right now.''

A FEW HOURS later, when Briana opened her condo's front door and smelled lemon-fresh polish combined with the fragrant odor of a homemade dinner, her thoughts weren't on her baby girls. She was thinking about Hunter and his trickery.

She was still angry with him, but the thought of a great meal and a clean place was nice.

''Alice?'' she called.

The lady Grace had introduced her to several months ago came out of the kitchen. ''Ms. McCallum. You're home. I hope you're hungry.''

''I'm starved, and something smells delicious. I hope coming so soon didn't cause you any problems?''

''No, ma'am. Frankly, I was ready for some company.'' The woman beamed at her.

''Why don't you join me for dinner and we'll talk? You might've had some trouble familiarizing yourself with my place.''

''Oh, I only fixed enough for one. You need to eat it all.''

Bri stepped into the kitchen and watched as Alice filled the table with food. She gulped, then said, ''Alice, when I said I was starving, I didn't mean I'd have this big an appetite. There will be plenty for both of us. In fact, I think you should eat dinner with me every evening before you go home. Unless you wouldn't like it. But some conversation would be nice, and there's no reason for you to cook twice.''

''I'd love it, if you don't mind. I'll pay for half the food,'' Alice assured her, her eyes big.

Bri laughed. ''As long as I don't have to fix it, I'll gladly pay for it.'' She pulled out a chair and sat down.

Alice joined her. After a few questions about how Briana liked her laundry done, Alice began asking her questions about her job and life at the hospital.

Before Bri knew it, they'd finished the meal, and she was completely relaxed. ''Alice, that was wonderful. I'm feeling more relaxed than I have in weeks. Thank you.''

''I'm glad you liked it. I enjoyed myself, too. Hearing about your job is like listening to a real live soap opera. Now, you go take your bath and get dressed for bed while I do the dishes. Then I can go home knowing that you're all settled in for the night.''

Obviously, Alice had been taking lessons from Grace, but Bri didn't complain. She only resisted when the orders came from Hunter. She had to resist the strong pull she felt from him. Being in his arms overpowered all her common sense.

''I could help with the dishes.''

"You've already worked all day. I'll take care of these."

Bri left the kitchen and went to soak in the tub. Afterward, she dressed in a long flannel gown. It was December, not cold, in Austin, but not warm, either. She pulled socks onto her feet and wandered back into the living room. One of her favorite shows was coming on. She settled among the cushions just as Alice brought her a cup of hot tea.

"Thank you, Alice. I love hot tea."

"That's what Grace said. This tea doesn't have any caffeine, so you can sleep well tonight. I'm going on home now unless there's anything else you want me to do."

"Oh, no, you've been wonderful. If you only want to come every other day, I'll be fine."

"I'd like to come back tomorrow, if you don't mind. I thought I'd bake some chicken for tomorrow's dinner. It's so nice to have someone to cook for."

"Fine with me," she agreed with a smile and bid the woman good-night. When Bri slid between clean sheets at ten o'clock, she sighed with pleasure. And Alice was coming every day. She sighed again.

She guessed she owed Hunter a thank-you for Alice, too, but she was getting tired of having to thank him all the time. Though she hadn't really gotten around to thanking him today.

Oh, well, she'd thank him tomorrow. If he didn't irritate her first.

THE HOSPITAL was abuzz the next morning. The first multiple births had occurred at 3:00 a.m. that morning. Twin boys were sleeping in the nursery, and most of the staff had taken time for a visit to look at the two small babies. They'd weighed in at 5 lbs. 9 oz. and 5 lbs. 4 oz.

As soon as Lisa told Bri about their arrival, Bri hurried to the first floor, where the nursery was located, to see them.

"Aren't they darling?" she asked without even looking to see who had come up beside her.

"Yes, they are," Maggie McCallum agreed, sadness in her voice.

"Maggie! I didn't even realize that was you. How are you doing?" Bri knew her sister-in-law wanted a baby badly.

"The same as ever," she said, offering a smile that wasn't very sincere.

Bri hugged her. "Dr. Sheppard is very good at her job. I'm sure if you give it time, you'll be all right."

"She says we will…if Adam cooperates."

Bri gave Maggie all her attention. "Is that brother of mine being difficult?" She knew Adam could be stubborn.

"He has to be tested and…you know how men are about that macho stuff." Maggie's cheeks turned pink. "I've tried to tell him it's probably all my fault but—"

"Maggie McCallum, don't you let him push you around. It's not either of your faults. Neither of you would keep from having a baby on purpose. Let Dr. Sheppard help you and soon you'll have one—or more—of your own.''

Maggie's eyes filled with tears. "I hope so," she whispered.

"Admiring our new residents?" Hunter asked as he stepped to Bri's side.

"Yes, of course," she said, hoping he wouldn't notice Maggie's distress.

He stuck his hand out and introduced himself.

Maggie took his hand and explained that she was Adam McCallum's wife.

"I haven't met Adam, yet, though I've had a couple of conversations with Caleb," Hunter explained.

Bri turned to stare at him. "Oh, really? A couple? When were they?"

She knew she'd just discovered his source for Grace's telephone number, but she didn't know what his other conversation with Caleb had been about. And she wanted to know.

"Um, just, er, casual conversations. He's a security consultant for the hospital, you know." Hunter tried a smile, then he turned to Maggie. "Do you work here, too?"

"No. I have an appointment with Dr. Sheppard."

"Great. She's a good doctor."

"You're not changing the subject, Dr. Callaghan," Bri said. "What else did you talk to Caleb about besides Grace's telephone number?"

Hunter replied, ''Just this and that. How long have you been married, Maggie?''

A man stepped forward, one with hazel eyes and brown hair. ''Long enough to know better than to flirt with strangers.'' His tone of voice told everyone he wasn't happy.

''Adam,'' Maggie said hurriedly. ''This is Dr. Callaghan, the new head of obstetrics. Dr. Callaghan, this is my husband, Adam McCallum. He and Bri were just talking about his conversations with Caleb.''

Though he still frowned, Adam seemed a little friendlier. ''You had lunch with Dad and Bri the day before yesterday, too.''

''Yes, I did. A nice lunch.''

''So what have you been talking to my brother about?''

''Just what I want to know, too,'' Bri said, her arms crossed.

Chapter Eleven

Hunter took his time giving an answer. "I like to talk to adult members of a multiple birth. I think it helps give me perspective. After meeting Bri and Caleb, I'm really glad I finally get to meet you."

"You think there's something wrong with people of multiple births?" Adam demanded.

"Not at all. In fact, sometimes I envy the bonding that children do in the womb. It seems to last a lifetime." He kept his gaze on Adam, but he could feel Bri bristling beside him. "Bri, for instance, is fiercely independent, but very close to both her brothers."

"That's true," Adam agreed. "How you doing, sis? Are the babies all right?"

"They're fine."

"Is Dr. Callaghan going to handle the delivery?" Maggie asked.

"Yes," Hunter said calmly.

"No!" Bri screamed at the same time. Adam and Maggie stared, and she hurriedly added, "Abby is my doctor. She'll handle the delivery."

Hunter smiled at her. "But I'll be there, too. I intend to attend all the multiple births until I become very familiar with my staff."

"You don't have to worry about Abby. She's the best."

"I'm sure she is," Hunter replied.

"I might have them at an inconvenient time," she added, realizing she hadn't convinced him.

"More inconvenient than three in the morning?" he asked, grinning. "That's when these guys put in an appearance."

"Who delivered them?" Bri asked.

"Dr. Beaumont. And he did a great job."

"Didn't he resent being watched?"

"I don't think so. We had breakfast together afterward."

"Bri," Adam added, his voice calm and reasonable, which only aggravated Bri more, "I'm sure Dr. Beaumont understood. After all, Dr. Callaghan has a job to do."

"You're just siding with him because you're a man! You and Caleb always did that!"

"Watch your blood pressure, honey," Hunter said softly.

But not softly enough.

"Honey?" Adam asked, frowning again.

"I have to go," Bri announced abruptly and left them all standing there, staring at her as she walked away.

When she reached her office, Lisa greeted her. "Hi,

Bri. I didn't know you'd met Dr. Callaghan before he arrived. Why didn't you say so?''

Bri's hands flew to her temples to massage the headache beginning to make itself felt. ''We didn't become good friends. We just met, that's all. No big deal.''

''But I guess that's why he's so friendly with you. After all, you're the only one he knew before he got here,'' Lisa said, beaming at Bri. ''So, I guess you've got the inside track.''

Bri stared at her. ''The inside track for what?''

''Dr. Callaghan. Half the staff wants to marry him. But when they hear you knew him before, they may all give up.''

Bri took a deep breath. ''Tell them not to give up, because I'm abandoning the track right now. I'm not exactly the shape for long-distance running.''

Bri started to walk past her, but Lisa raised her eyebrows and said, ''The question isn't your behavior but Dr. Callaghan's. He already acts like he's hooked.''

Bri rubbed her temples again. ''Lisa, I don't want to discuss this subject ever again. And do what you can to discourage anyone else from doing so. There is *nothing* between me and Dr. Callaghan. Okay?'' Then she stomped into her office.

''Okay,'' she heard Lisa say. She hoped Lisa meant that answer as a promise to help curtail the speculation about a romance. But Bri was afraid her agitated reaction might cause even more speculation.

And darn it! She still hadn't thanked the man!

E-mail! She was going to deal with him through e-mail. She could be calm and reasonable when she didn't have to talk to him.

She immediately wrote a gracious—well, not too gracious—note thanking him for keeping an eye on her. She reminded him that she was a professional and hoped he would treat her as one.

Then she lay back in her chair, taking deep breaths and closing her eyes. Her checkup with Abby was in half an hour. She didn't want her blood pressure to alarm Abby.

"ABBY? This is Hunter. I'm planning on sitting in on Bri's checkup. Helen told you, didn't she?"

"Yes, of course, Hunter."

"Look, don't be alarmed about Bri's blood pressure. And take it before you tell her I'm coming. I'm going to wait outside until she's on the table, prepped for the ultrasound."

"Is something wrong?" Abby asked cautiously.

"She got upset this morning. She felt her brother sided with me on something and it upset her."

"She seems particularly sensitive to—well, to you."

Hunter couldn't think of what to say.

"I heard she met you at a conference."

It was Hunter's turn to be silent. He hadn't realized she'd told anyone that. "Uh, yes, briefly. We didn't really get to know each other."

"Which conference did you meet at?"

"I don't know. I'd have to check my calendar. Does it matter?" He didn't give her a chance to answer. "Look, she's embarrassed to have me observe the checkup because we're acquaintances. It'd be like having your brother-in-law watch you undress. We just need to keep her calm. When you're ready to start the sonogram, knock on the door. I'll be waiting just outside."

"All right, fine."

He waited until five minutes after Bri's appointment time before he slipped into Abby's outer office in the main hospital. Bri wasn't in the waiting room.

The receptionist assured him Bri was already in an exam room, so he asked to talk to Abby's nurse. As he'd hoped, Abby had left instructions.

"She said you were going to wait outside the door. Peggy, the other nurse, is with the two of them."

"Just show me which room they're in," he said softly.

He felt sure Abby had planned the ultrasound for the last part of the checkup. He was eager to see his daughters.

He stood at the door for several minutes, hearing the murmur of feminine voices. Then a soft knock informed him he could enter.

Stepping into the room, he nodded to Abby and walked to the head of the table. Bri was staring at the monitor, probably assuming he was another nurse. But something must have alerted her to his presence, and she shrieked and dove for the sheet, trying to cover her stomach.

"What are you doing here?" she demanded in a hoarse whisper.

"I want to see the ultrasound, both to check the babies and to evaluate the quality of the machine. Abby agreed."

"Well, someone should've asked me. I don't want you here." She turned to Abby. "Please, Abby, make him leave!"

Abby stepped forward and took her hand. "Bri, you're all covered up except for your stomach, and I'm sure Dr. Callaghan has seen pregnant stomachs before. Just relax before your blood pressure gets too high. Your babies need more time in the womb. Take deep breaths."

Hunter spoke softly to the nurse and she left the room.

"Do you need something?" Abby asked, frowning.

"Yeah, something to bring down the blood pressure," Hunter said.

"I don't think medication—" Abby began as the nurse came back into the room carrying a towel and a bottle of lotion.

"Of course not. But a foot rub will do the trick," he said, pouring cream into his hand.

"What did he say? What's he doing?" Bri asked, trying to raise her head high enough to see over her stomach. Then she sighed as he began rubbing cream on her feet. After a moment, she remembered to protest. "Hunter, you shouldn't—"

"Relax, Bri. Abby's going to show us those three little girls. Let's have a look-see." Then he nodded to Abby as he continued to massage Bri's feet.

He only stopped once, when the picture first clearly showed his three little girls. "They're beautiful," he murmured, and received an enthusiastic agreement from Abby.

Bri, lying more relaxed on the table, blinked away tears, but her gaze was focused on the screen that showed three squirmy babies jockeying for position in their limited space.

After a quick look at Bri, Hunter began massaging her feet again, silently giving thanks that Bri had decided to keep their children and try to manage on her own. She was a courageous woman. Even if she wanted nothing to do with him after the babies were born, he felt sure she wouldn't stop him from seeing the girls.

"Everything's all right?" Bri asked Abby, sniffing away the tears.

"Oh, they're doing beautifully, Bri. And if you give birth now, they'll make it just fine. But the longer you carry them, the faster they'll go home from the hospital."

"I'm being careful." Then, she flashed her gaze to Hunter and back to Abby. "I've already hired a lady to help at home, so I can get plenty of rest."

"Oh, good. I'd been worrying about how much you were trying to do. Good decision."

Bri's gaze returned to Hunter. "Yes. I appreciated the concern that—I got some good advice."

Slowly, he grinned, knowing that was her way of thanking him. Pretty magnanimous, since he'd been interfering where he had no right to interfere. Maybe she would accept his protection a little more readily in the future.

Even as he was thinking such pleasant thoughts, her jaw firmed and her lips were pressed together. "But I'm an adult, and I can manage my affairs by myself."

He had no intention of letting her try—no matter what she said!

THAT EVENING was again delightful. Alice joined Bri for dinner, and everything in her house was sparkling and fresh.

"You're going to have to mess up more things, young lady, so I'll have enough to do."

"Oh, Alice, you shouldn't be working so hard."

"Well, I wanted to ask you about cooking ahead. Most things are good for six months, I think. I thought I'd bake some lasagna and freeze it. Maybe a cake or two, because you'll probably have several visitors after the babies are born. We'll need something to feed them when they visit."

"That's a wonderful idea, Alice, if you don't mind the extra work."

"Well, I have the time now. If you don't mind the added expense."

Bri quickly assured her she didn't. After dinner she took a shower. Abby had suggested it might be best to have showers now. Then she settled among the cushions on the sofa, turned on the television and relaxed. Alice brought her a cup of tea and some cookies.

"I'm not sure I should eat the cookies."

"Dr. Callaghan said you need to fatten up a little so your babies won't be too skinny."

Bri froze. "When did Dr. Callaghan say that?"

"He told me today when he called to tell me your checkup went well. He knew I'd be worried and he was afraid you wouldn't want to talk about it."

Though she was fuming inside, Bri tried to make her voice calm. "I'm sorry, I didn't think to tell you. But everyone's fine."

"I know," Alice said with a smile. "Now eat your cookies and drink your tea. I put in cream instead of milk. It makes it taste wonderful."

Alice was so pleased with her behavior, Bri couldn't be mad at her. But she could be mad at Dr. Hunter Callaghan.

As soon as Alice left, she grabbed the phone. She wasn't calling Hunter. Not yet. She had some other calls to make.

"Dad? Just wanted to let you know that my checkup went well."

"Yes, I'm so glad. Hunter said the girls looked

great. He thinks you may make it almost to term. I really appreciated his letting me know. I've been worrying about you.''

''So why didn't you call me?''

After a moment of heavy silence, Jackson said, ''I was afraid you'd get scared because I was worried. After what happened to your mother, you know.''

Tears filled her eyes. ''I know, Dad. But it's all right. We have better doctors and better equipment, thanks to you. Everything is going to be fine.''

''Yeah, Hunter assured me he'd take care of you and the girls.'' He actually sniffed into the phone, as if he were hiding tears, as she had in the doctor's office. ''Hey, how about lunch again tomorrow?''

''Thanks, Dad, but with the appointment today, I lost a lot of work time, so I can't go out for lunch. I'll just have my assistant bring me something. I'll take a rain check if you don't mind.''

''Okay, but you let me know if there's anything you need.''

''I will, Dad.''

When she'd disconnected, she began dialing Caleb's number, but a knock on her door stopped her. She moved to the door to peek through the peephole. Dr. Hunter Callaghan, bossy doctor, stood there.

She was wearing her Hawaiian muumuu, so she swung open the door, a big glare on her face.

''Hmm, welcome as usual,'' he said with a grin.

''How dare you!''

''I don't know how I dare, since I don't know

what's got you steamed this time. Unless it's my sitting in on your checkup.''

"No! I've accepted that you have a right to do that, though I don't like it." She folded her arms across her chest, though they actually rested on top of her stomach. "But you don't have a right to interfere in my personal life."

He nudged her backward and stepped inside, closing the door. She was so wrapped up in her anger, she didn't realize what he'd done for several minutes. "I didn't invite you in!"

"But you should have. Grace would be appalled at your manners," he assured her, still smiling.

"You think you're so smart, but you wouldn't be so popular if I told everyone you abandoned me after getting me pregnant!"

She immediately realized what she'd done when his eyes brightened and he took a step closer. "I didn't mean *you* really—I meant what if I told them that! That's what I meant. What if I lied to them?"

Somewhere during that speech, he'd switched to doctor mode, instead of father-to-be mode. "Your blood pressure is rising again. Come sit down. I'll make you some more tea."

"How do you know I want tea? Maybe I want a slug of whiskey, or a soda, or Kool-Aid! You don't know me—or what I want."

"I know you don't want to hurt your babies. Come sit down, Bri."

He arranged cushions behind her back. Then he

picked up her cup and took it to the kitchen. In no time he was back with a fresh cup of tea, with cream added, much as Alice had made.

"Do you still have cookies to eat?" he asked.

She glared at him and didn't answer.

"Honey, we need to talk about what's upset you so it won't make your blood pressure go up. I promise I haven't deliberately tried to rile you." He sat on the couch, pressing against her legs as she lay there. "Now, tell me what I did this time."

"You told Alice, my dad, and probably Adam, Caleb and Grace about my checkup." She doubled up her fist and hit him in the arm, knowing it wouldn't hurt him, but maybe it would let him know how angry she was. "Alice told me I needed to eat the cookies because you told her I needed calories."

"Who else but your cook should I have told? And I had to tell her about seeing the babies, so she'd believe me."

"And my father?"

"Well, I could tell, when we talked at lunch, he was putting up a front about everything being all right. He was scared to death you were going to die just as your mother did. I wanted to reassure him."

Her eyes filled with tears, and she bit her bottom lip. "And my brothers?"

"Your father asked me to call and reassure them because they were worried sick about you, too. You're the only female in the group. They don't know if you're just trying to reassure them, or if maybe you don't know what's going to happen.''

''And they believe you because you're a man!''

''No, they believe me because I'm a medical professional who's delivered a lot of babies.''

''Did you call Grace, too?''

''Yes, because she asked me to. She said she didn't like to ask you because she was afraid it would make you worry.''

She sniffed. She'd been sure the man had overstepped his mark, but there he was, explaining it all away, making her look like a hysterical woman. ''I— I still think you should've at least told me you were going to—to interfere in my life.''

He leaned forward to pick up the cup of tea and then held it to her lips. ''Take a sip.''

She did so, trying to ignore his body pressed against her stomach. His touch drove her crazy. It apparently affected the girls, too, because they suddenly began jumping around like five-year-olds playing soccer, running in all directions and kicking anything that moved.

After he set the cup back on the table, he looked at her and whispered, ''May I?''

She didn't have to ask what he wanted. She knew he wanted to feel her babies move. She nodded.

His big warm hands spread out over her stomach, acting like a lightning rod for the movement. One lump in particular caught his attention. ''I think one of the girls is standing on her head.'' He rubbed the lump and it shifted.

''They move around a lot, especially at night.''

''Bri, I want to thank you for having the courage not to terminate the pregnancy.''

''You're wel—I mean, it has nothing to do with you! Nothing at all.''

With his hands still on her stomach, he stared at her, challenging her words.

''These are my girls, and no one, not their father or anyone, is going to hurt my girls.''

''Why would you think their father would want to hurt them?'' he asked softly.

''Because he hurt me! He left me alone, wanting—wanting his love and—and my children are better off just belonging to me. I won't hurt them.''

''Are we talking about the mythical boyfriend who split? Or are we talking about me?''

She looked away, refusing to give him an answer. ''I'm tired. I want to go to sleep.''

He sighed. ''Okay. Do you need a foot rub?''

''No! I can manage.''

''All right, but you need to understand, Bri, that I'm going to watch over you, try to care for you and the girls. I'm not trying to hurt you or trap you into anything, okay?''

''Fine.''

''Okay, I'm going to go turn down the covers. Take my arm while I walk you to your bedroom.''

''I can—''

"I know you can. Just let me help. Then I'll lock the door as I leave."

"Fine!"

They walked to her bedroom in silence. He pulled down the covers, then covered her up as she settled in the bed. As he turned away, she saw him pause by her dresser.

"What is it?" she demanded as he picked something up and looked at it. Frantically, she tried to think what he could've found. Whatever it was, he put it back in the ceramic bowl where he'd found it and told her good-night. The minute he'd left her bedroom, she knew what he'd found.

A black stud from a tuxedo—ripped from Hunter the night they'd made love. The one thing she'd found of Hunter's the next morning.

And treasured. The one sign that what she'd experienced hadn't been a figment of her imagination.

Even if he *had* left her.

Chapter Twelve

Hunter left Bri's condo with a smile on his face. For the first time, Bri had admitted the girls were his daughters. She'd given it away when she'd threatened to tell everyone he'd abandoned her.

He was coming to know Bri better, and he was pretty sure she told the truth. Except to him.

When he'd seen the tuxedo stud, he knew it was the one he'd been unable to find the morning he'd left her room. And she'd kept it. And she'd said the father of her babies had abandoned her when she'd wanted him to love her.

She wanted him to love her.

He was willing. But he was pretty sure she couldn't handle any pressure about her life right now. It was taking a lot of work on his part to keep her blood pressure from rising too high. The best thing he could do now was to take care of her and the girls. Later, when they were safely born, he'd woo her, convince her he hadn't left her.

The last thing he'd wanted was to lose her. He

climbed into his SUV and looked up at her windows, dark now so she could sleep. If he was lucky, he'd get his cake and eat it, too. He'd have Bri to love and three little girls to complete his life.

All he had to do was wait.

THE NEXT MORNING, the tenth of December, Bri got to work early. The hospital opening had occurred before Hunter had arrived. She hadn't wanted Christmas decorations up until after the opening.

Today they would be hanging two angels in maroon robes with golden halos on their heads, playing their horns, in the huge windows of the lobby. The angels would be seen both from inside and outside the hospital.

At the other end of the lobby, there would be a huge Christmas tree, a real one. The fragrant scent of pine would fill the air. Twinkling white lights would cover the tree, as well as oversized ornaments.

All the departments would get a regular-sized artificial tree. Though Bri hated to use the artificial ones, she did because some patients might be allergic to the smell of real evergreens. The staff members would decorate their trees. Overnight, the entire hospital was going to be festive.

She loved Christmas.

"Bri, nice job," April called as she crossed the lobby at eight. "I wondered when we would have decorations."

"I wanted to wait until after the opening. By then it was hard to get on the schedule," Bri explained.

"This is perfect. We'll have at least a couple of weeks to enjoy them. How'd your checkup go yesterday?"

"Fine," Bri said, thinking that at least here was one person Hunter hadn't called. "Abby says the girls are in good shape if we have to deliver any time soon, but late January is still the expected delivery."

"Great. I heard we got several more patients in the hospital last night. Let's go to the cafeteria and have some breakfast, and I'll tell you all about it."

"Did Hunter put you up to this?"

She regretted her question when April looked at her with surprise.

"No. I didn't eat breakfast. All I could think about all the way here were those cinnamon rolls Sam makes. Don't you love them?"

With a sigh, Bri agreed. "Yeah. Let me tell the guys where I'll be if they run into any problems." She consulted the workers and then followed April to the cafeteria.

Soon she was indulging in a cup of hot tea and a big cinnamon bun, warmed to just the right temperature. "I'd worry about the calories, but Hunter is encouraging me to eat more."

"Wow! That's my kind of doctor. I thought Abby was your ob-gyn, though."

"Uh, yeah. Dr. Callaghan is a hands-on supervisor."

"I see." After taking a bite, April looked at her friend. "There are a lot of rumors circling the wing."

"About what?" Bri asked cautiously.

"About you and Dr. Callaghan."

Bri chewed deliberately on her bite of cinnamon bun, giving herself time to answer. "Don't believe anything you hear. People make things up," she said with a big smile.

The level of noise in the room mounted, and they both turned around to see what had caused the uproar. Two men brought in big boxes and began putting together the artificial Christmas tree for the cafeteria. It was bigger than most of the trees because the room was so large.

"I guess everyone's pleased about the decorations," Bri said, delighted to change the conversational topic.

"Yeah, some of them thought we wouldn't have Christmas decorations this first year, since we had the big opening."

"Oh, no! I should've said something. That didn't occur to me. I just didn't want them up until after the opening, that's all."

"I know. But it's going to lift the spirits of everyone. And having the new patients will, too."

"You haven't told me about them."

"One lady is having twins, but her blood pressure got too high. Her doctor thought she would carry them longer if she remained in bed."

"Oh," Bri groaned. She hoped that didn't happen to her.

"The other is a teenager. She'd been living at a boardinghouse nearby. Dr. Beaumont got her on the approved list for a charity case and they moved her in last night. She's only a little over six months and she's carrying quadruplets. I've heard they're small. She didn't get any prenatal care until she saw Dr. Beaumont a couple of days ago."

Bri shuddered. "That's terrible. I hope the babies make it."

"Yeah, I think they said she's twenty-six weeks, so she's three or four weeks behind you."

"Well, I'd better finish my breakfast and get upstairs. I'll want to be sure they have everything they need for both patients. But I'll stop and check on the twins we already have in the nursery. Aren't they sweet?" Bri asked.

"They're terrific, and already gaining weight. I think they and their mom will go home tomorrow," April said. "Our first successful multiple birth for the wing."

"Okay. I'll see you later."

After checking on the twins and stopping in their mother's room to see if she had any complaints, Bri went back to the lobby to make sure everything was progressing as it should.

The foreman came over to speak with her. "Ms. McCallum, the new head doctor wanted us to add a banner that says Peace on Earth beneath the angels.

We have a really nice one with gold-leaf trim that looks as if it's on a roll, but it will cost an extra five hundred. He said to ask you about the expense.''

The budget was tight, but she decided to grant Hunter's request. Everyone was so excited about the decorations. It made her feel guilty that she hadn't let them know they would have Christmas decorations before now.

''All right, that will be fine. Just add it to our bill.''

''Great. It will look real nice.''

''I'm sure it will.''

On the way to her office, she was humming ''Silent Night'' beneath her breath. She stopped by Hunter's office and told Helen to assure Dr. Callaghan they were adding Peace on Earth. ''He'll know what I mean, Helen.''

''Is that Bri?'' Hunter called from his office.

''Maybe you'd better tell him yourself, Bri. He'll be upset if you try to avoid him.''

Bri raised her eyebrows, unused to not being obeyed by the employees, but she guessed Helen didn't want to be caught between the two of them. She crossed over to Hunter's door. ''Yes, it's me. I just wanted to tell you that we're adding Peace on Earth.''

''Good. I think that will be a nice touch.''

''Thank you for leaving the decision up to me.''

He grinned. ''No problem. You heard about our two new patients?''

''Yes, I'm checking with their doctors to see if they

have everything they need. I suspect the teenager might need a few things."

"Can we provide them?"

"It will get done," she said, not mentioning that the money might come out of her own pocket. She was fortunate to have the funds to live as she wanted. She liked to help those who couldn't.

"If you need a donation, let me know."

"Okay, thanks."

"Oh, and Bri? Nice working with you."

He was right. This was the first time they'd both wanted the same thing. And it was nice. She gave him a smile and slipped away.

After calls to the two doctors of the new patients, Bri went back downstairs to visit with the teenager, Jenny Barrows. As she'd expected, the girl had almost nothing in the way of personal supplies. Afterward, Bri talked to the nurses.

"She didn't bring much with her. We put her in a hospital gown because she didn't have anything but a T-shirt."

"And she has no family," the second nurse added.

"All right. We'll see if we can help her out a little," Bri said.

Both nurses relaxed. "Thanks, Bri. That's great."

She returned to her office. "Lisa, we're going shopping. Switch the phones to voice mail because we'll be gone a while."

An hour later, they returned from one of the large economy stores, with several bags. "Why don't you take off the price tags and go introduce yourself to Jenny, our new patient, and tell her these things are hers to keep.''

"But Bri, you should take them. You bought them."

"The charity fund bought them. I'll fill in an expense-account form for the money. Besides, I need to check all the departments to be sure the trees are taken care of.''

"But I could do that and save you some—''

"Just do as I ask, Lisa," she said quietly. "I'm going to eat lunch before I check the departments, so it will be a while before I get back.''

"Yes, ma'am. I'll switch the phones back on as soon as I return.''

"Good.''

After Lisa left, Bri drew a deep breath, then headed to the cafeteria. She was tired from the shopping expedition, which probably explained why she didn't shop anymore.

After she'd chosen her meal, she turned around to look for an empty table. She found one near the windows and sat down with a sigh. No question about her appetite today.

"Mind if I join you?'' a male voice asked.

"Uh, I don't mind, but it would be better if you don't. There's a lot of gossip already," she told Hunter, giving him a quick glance and then staring at her plate.

"I told you not to pay any attention to gossip," he said lightly, sliding his tray onto the table beside her.

Bri was concerned about the thrill that seemed to flow through her. She mustn't let her hormones dictate her behavior. She had to think of the girls. And her weak resistance when it came to Hunter. She was as hard as whipped cream when it came to Hunter. Then she caught sight of Annabelle just leaving the cash register. She waved to get her friend's attention.

"You don't mind if my friend joins us, do you?" Bri asked, staring at Hunter.

"Of course not. I'm hoping to get familiar with all the staff."

Annabelle reached the table.

"Join us, Annabelle," Bri said at once, pleading with her eyes.

"Of course, if Dr. Callaghan doesn't mind." Annabelle kept looking from one to the other as she sat down after Hunter's assurance that she was welcome.

"Dr. Callaghan, this is Annabelle Reardon. She's one of our delivery nurses."

"Of course, that's where I've seen you. You were there when the twins were delivered."

"Yes, that's right."

"Good job. You work with Dr. Beaumont a lot?"

"When I can. He's a good doctor."

The two of them continued to chat, and Bri found it easier to eat her food. She could see Hunter watching her to see if she ate, but she could ignore that.

"Oh, Bri, the Christmas decorations are so wonderful. We weren't sure—"

"I should have explained to everyone. As soon as I can, I'm going to put out a weekly newsletter that will keep everyone posted on what's going on."

"Good idea," Hunter said, and Bri was pleased.

"It won't happen any time soon, what with the babies coming."

"Why not ask the public relations department?" Hunter asked. "You can provide any information you want in the newsletters to them, but they could add birthdays, events in the lives of the staff, things everyone would be interested in."

"Do you think they'd have time?" Bri asked, pondering his idea.

"More than you. Besides, that falls under their expertise."

"That's a good idea," Annabelle said, beaming at Hunter.

Bri suddenly wondered if her friend was one of those members of the staff who was interested in Hunter. Not that she minded. Of course not.

"Annabelle's right about the decorations. You did a fine job, Bri. Have you already decorated at home?"

Bri ducked her head. "No. I probably won't this Christmas. It's a lot of work." She couldn't keep the longing out of her voice, but she figured the other two wouldn't notice.

Since she'd been eating while the other two talked, she finished her meal before them. "I hope you don't mind, but I need to check the Christmas trees in each department.''

''Can't someone else do that?'' Hunter asked, frowning.

''There's no need for someone else. I need to talk to the staff a little and apologize for not letting them know we were decorating,'' Bri said, then she slipped away.

HUNTER WATCHED Bri hurry away. They'd got along better today, and it had been nice. But she was still working too hard.

''Dr. Callaghan?''

''Yes, Annabelle, and make it Hunter. No need to be formal when it's just staff.''

''Oh, thank you. I need to ask you something. You sat in on Bri's last examination, didn't you?''

''Yes.'' He wondered what she wanted to know and whether Bri would get upset.

''I was going to ask Abby, but since you're here— You see, we're going to give Bri a shower. Well, April is, but several of us are helping her. We want to wait until January because Christmas is such a busy time, but we're worried she won't carry the babies that long. What do you think?''

Hunter smiled at the young woman. ''That's a tough call, but I don't think she'll go full term. I'm hoping we can get her through New Year's.''

''Oh! Then we'd better have it right away. Thanks for the advice.'' She picked up her tray and stood.

"I've got to check in with Dr. Beaumont. He's going to look at Jenny Barrows again. He doesn't think she'll go much longer." She started to leave, then added, "I forgot to tell Bri how sweet it was that she went shopping for Jenny. The poor child has nothing."

"Bri's a generous woman."

"She's the best," Annabelle said with emphasis. Then she, too, abandoned him.

Bri had gone shopping this morning and now was touring the entire wing. She was going to be very tired tonight. He could call Alice and tell her to put Bri to bed at once, serving her dinner there. But Bri would get irritated again, and being in an almost civil relationship was quite pleasant. And gave him hope for later.

He remembered the longing in her voice for Christmas decorations. He didn't believe she could decorate even if she wanted to. Especially not after today's demands.

Maybe tomorrow would be easier. And she could sleep late on Saturday. If he carried everything to her apartment—then she might do a favor for him.

A smile settled on his face.

BRI WAS RELIEVED when she left the hospital Friday afternoon. Two days ahead of her of doing nothing but taking naps. Then she'd be able to face her job again on Monday. But it was getting more difficult to last through the week. She might have to admit that she needed to cut back.

Alice had certainly helped, but the days seemed longer recently.

Alice had fried chicken waiting when Bri arrived home. "Fried chicken? Doesn't that have too much fat and cholesterol?" she asked.

"It's not fried. It just looks and tastes that way. It's a special coating I put on it. My husband had high cholesterol and he hated baked chicken. I came up with this recipe," Alice said, beaming with pride.

"I can't wait to taste it. And I'm so glad it's Friday," she added.

"Sit down at the table, and I'll serve dinner at once."

But Bri noticed that Alice checked her watch.

"Alice, do you need to leave early? It's okay, I can serve myself."

"Aren't you a sweet thing. But, no, I don't have to leave. I just—"

The doorbell interrupted Alice and Bri realized that was what Alice had been waiting for. She was expecting someone.

Somehow it wasn't a surprise when she heard Hunter's voice. But there were some extra sounds she couldn't identify. Before she could decide to get up and do some investigating, Alice, followed by Hunter, entered the kitchen.

"Look who's here!" Alice said, pretending to be

surprised. "I asked him to join us since I had plenty of chicken made. You don't mind do you?"

"Of course not. How convenient that you made extra chicken."

Hunter sent her a rueful smile. "Alice, I don't think we fooled her. The truth is, Bri, Alice and I talked, and I told her I was going to do something for you in hopes that you'd help me. She asked me to dinner then."

Alice looked worried, and Bri couldn't upset her. "It's all right, Alice. We'd never turn down a hungry man."

"Kind of like helping Jenny Barrows," he said, raising one eyebrow.

Without looking at him, she said, "I'll file an expense account to cover that."

"Sure you will. You don't lie any better than Alice, Bri. The two of you are quite a pair."

Alice giggled, and even Bri couldn't hold back a smile.

"I'll practice," she said.

"Don't bother. You're perfect the way you are." After smiling at her, he turned to Alice. "Now, where's that special chicken, Alice? I'm starving."

Dinner was enjoyable. Hunter charmed both her and Alice, teasing them. Bri was glad Alice was there. It meant she wouldn't give in to the attraction that was the reason she was big as a house.

"This chicken is the best, Alice. You are a great cook."

"Wait until you try dessert. It's my special recipe for peach cobbler, still warm, with ice cream on top."

Hunter groaned. "I may have to deal with something else first. Then I'll have room for dessert."

"Something else?" Bri asked, frowning. "What something else?"

"Have you finished eating?"

"Yes."

"Then come with me. I have a surprise for you."

He took her hand and pulled her from her chair. Then he led her toward the living room.

By the time they reached the doorway, she already suspected what her surprise was. Standing in the corner was a full, fragrant Scotch pine tree, all ready for decorating.

Tears gathered in Bri's eyes.

He made it so hard to resist his care, his sweetness. He seemed to know her better than she knew herself. But that couldn't be true or he'd realize he only had to walk in the door to make her happy. Unless she remembered his abandonment.

Chapter Thirteen

Bri was back on the couch, among the pillows, her cup of hot tea in front of her. But she wasn't alone. Hunter and Alice were hanging ornaments on her Christmas tree.

She loved Christmas and all its trappings. This year, she'd thought she would have to give it all up. Just thinking about decorating a tree or doing anything other than the bare minimum made her tired.

But watching someone else do it was pure heaven.

Hunter turned and smiled at her. She smiled back. Perhaps she'd misjudged him. What if he had come back to her room, only to find her gone? It was possible. A sensitive, thoughtful man, as he was proving himself to be, wouldn't have simply walked away from her.

When he'd found out she was pregnant, the first thing he'd done was offer her marriage. Not a marriage of love, but at least he'd offered marriage.

She'd turned him down.

Did she wish now she still had that option?

Maybe, she admitted with a sigh.

"Tired, Bri? Do you want to go to bed? We can finish tomorrow or some other time."

Hunter again being thoughtful...and sensitive to her needs.

"No, I'm fine. I was just thinking how wonderful it is to have a Christmas tree. Thank you so much, Hunter."

"No problem. I'm having fun. I think Alice is doing all the work," he teased, winking at the house-keeper.

"No such thing. I wasn't going to decorate this year, since I'm all alone, but it does lift the spirits, doesn't it?"

"Yes, it does," Bri agreed.

But her mind remained on thoughts of Hunter. If she told him now she wanted to marry him, what would he say? She already knew. He'd agree at once, because he believed the girls were his babies. He'd agree, and she'd always fear she'd trapped him into marriage.

She couldn't do that to him.

"Uh, Bri, you haven't asked about the favor I'm hoping you'll do for me." Hunter said as he hung the last ornament on the tree.

Bri stared at him as he bent to plug in the lights. Suddenly the shadowy room was lit up with twinkling lights. She figured it didn't much matter what he asked. She'd agree to anything to thank him for his gift. "What?"

"Tomorrow afternoon, a real estate woman is showing me three houses. I'm going to need some advice. Would you come with me? I promise we won't be gone more than two or three hours. And I'll provide dinner."

"You want *my* advice? But I don't know what kind of lifestyle you have. I don't even know your favorite color," she pointed out.

He sat on the arm of the sofa beside her. "Hazel is my favorite color," he said, staring into her eyes.

"I would've thought blue to match your eyes."

"Blue was my favorite color until last spring."

She felt her cheeks flushing. "My dad might be a better choice. He knows the real estate market better than me."

"That's why I'm using a real estate agent. Please, Bri? I promise I won't let you get too tired."

"I suppose—I mean, I'll be glad to help you. Especially since you brought me my tree. I just thought there might be others who would be able to provide better advice."

He leaned down and kissed her cheek. "Nope. You'll have the best advice for me."

Bri hadn't even realized Alice had left the room until she reentered with a tray. On it were two desserts, hot tea for Bri and decaf coffee for Hunter.

"I'm not having dessert, so I think I'll go home now, if that's all right. Just put the dishes in the sink and I'll take care of them tomorrow," Alice commented.

"Thank you, Alice," Hunter said.

"Alice, I can't thank you enough for helping Hunter with the tree and for the wonderful dinner," Bri added.

"I enjoyed it. Do you want me to come in tomorrow?"

"On Saturday? Absolutely not. You enjoy your weekend."

Alice left and Hunter served Bri's dessert to her.

"Are these calories I need, too?" she asked.

"Yes. After looking at that teenager's babies, I definitely want you to eat well. You *are* taking your vitamins, aren't you?"

"Of course I am," she said before taking her first bite of cobbler. "Oh, my, Alice is a good cook."

"Yes, she is."

"Hunter, are Jenny's babies in bad shape?" They all knew the risks with multiple births, but it would be demoralizing to lose babies so early after the wing's opening. Or any time for that matter. She wanted the McCallum Wing to save every baby.

Hunter sighed. "Well, they're okay…right now. But they are small. And if she delivers right away, it will be touch and go. Zach is hoping for another couple of weeks."

"Christmas?"

"We'll be lucky if she makes it that long."

"Will I make it that long?"

He grinned. "I've told the girls they'll still get

presents if they wait until New Year's. Is that okay with you?''

"Oh, yes," she agreed with a sigh. "New Year's would be perfect.''

HUNTER HAD BEEN in the hotel almost a week. The changes in his life had happened quickly. He'd decided to wait a few days before he committed to Austin by buying a house.

But once he'd discovered Bri's pregnancy, he'd known he'd be living in Austin for a long time. Unless she agreed to move away with him.

He'd called a Realtor a few days ago and given her very specific requirements for a house. He'd also begun applying for a loan. The Realtor had assured him that the three homes she wanted him to see today would meet his requirements.

Strangely, he felt nervous when he picked up Bri. Buying a house was a major move in life, and he wanted one that would hold his future with ease. His future was Bri.

"How are you feeling this morning?" he asked as he led her to his SUV. After opening the door, he lifted her onto the high seat.

"Fine," she said, a little flustered by his assistance. It was becoming obvious to her that she loved Hunter's touch. "I slept late."

"Good. But you ate breakfast and lunch, didn't you?"

"Yes, mother hen, I ate everything in sight. And that's a lot since Alice started working for me."

"She's working out well, isn't she?"

"Yes, thanks to someone's good advice I'm having a much easier time of it now." Her smile warmed him as he circled the SUV and got behind the wheel.

Then she changed the subject. "Where are the houses we're going to look at?"

"All three are in the hills. Once of them looks down on Town Lake. And, surprisingly, they're not too far from the hospital."

"Sounds like Dad's and Adam's neighborhood."

"They live close together? Does that work out all right?"

"Oh, yes. They don't see each other all that often because both Dad and Adam are workaholics. Caleb, on the other hand, has a condo, like me. He's a loner, I guess. I worry about him."

Hunter grinned. "That's what being a family is. Worry. And joy."

He then told her stories about his family and their concern for each other. "Dad's the worst, since Mom's gone. But he'd do anything for either my brother or me. He's going to ship all my belongings down when I get a place."

"It must be hard living out of a suitcase," she murmured with sympathy.

"Not really. But I'm looking forward to having my own place again. Maybe when I do, I can hire Alice away from you."

"Oh, no, I can't let you do that!" she exclaimed, laughing.

She thought he was teasing. But he intended them to share Alice...in one house...after the babies came.

"Here's the first one," he said as he pulled to a halt in front of a large home.

"Isn't this rather large for one person?" she asked, frowning.

He shrugged his shoulders, not willing to explain what he had in mind. It would just throw her into a rise in blood pressure.

They met the Realtor and walked through the house with her. Then she gave them the address of the second house and they followed her to it. Again they walked through. While Bri admired both houses, Hunter didn't see any real enthusiasm in her face.

"Where is the third?" he asked, getting discouraged.

"It's the one that looks down on Town Lake. I'll admit it's my favorite," the Realtor said.

Hunter mentally crossed his fingers. He wanted to get a house right away and have it ready for his family when he convinced Bri to move in with him.

The instant they drove up to the last house, he would've signed a contract.

Bri's eyes lit up and she softly sighed, "Oh, my. How beautiful."

"Yeah. I can't wait to see the inside."

It was perfect. A large, welcoming home. It even had a downstairs bedroom off the kitchen which would be perfect for Alice. Four bedrooms upstairs, so each girl would eventually have her own room, and the parents would be nearby. Large closets, lots of baths and a huge family room downstairs.

"This house is perfect, but I'm afraid you'd rattle around in it by yourself," Bri warned.

"Maybe someday I'll have a family." He watched Bri's face as he said that, hoping to see a touch of jealousy.

"Yes, of course. I—you're right. This house will be perfect."

"You like the kitchen? I think that's one of the most important rooms in a house."

"No one could complain about this kitchen. It's huge with the breakfast room a part of it. It would be a great gathering place for a family. In fact, don't show it to Alice or you *might* be able to hire her away from me." She gave him a wobbly smile that made him want to hold her against him, to comfort her, to love her.

He hurriedly turned away. The Realtor had discreetly stepped into the hallway to give them time to confer. Hunter called her over. "I want this house. Can I make an offer today?"

"Of course. The couple had to move quickly and they're motivated to sell. I'll call them as soon as I get back to the office. What do you want to offer?"

Hunter didn't dicker too much. He figured the house would sell quickly, and he wanted to be the one who got it.

Bri joined him as they got ready to leave.

The Realtor smiled at her. "You're going to love this house. I hope you get it."

Bri flashed him a quick look, then said, "I hope Hunter gets it, too. It's lovely."

"But I thought—uh, yes. Me, too."

They got back in the SUV and she turned to him.

"She thought—"

"I know. People assume things. After all, you don't look like a swinging single, Briana, you'll have to admit."

"No, I look like one who swung…and got caught," she said with a rueful laugh.

"Not by yourself." When she didn't respond to that, he added, "I love the house. Thanks for coming with me."

"Oh, I'm glad I did. The view from the family room of Town Lake is incredible."

"I'll let you know when I get word. How tired are you?"

"I'm fine."

"You always say that. Do you feel up to dinner out at a restaurant, or do you want me to get some take-out dinner and we can eat at your place?"

"I'm up for a restaurant. It won't be long before they ban me in case I break a chair, so I'd better enjoy eating out while I can. After the babies come, it will be impossible. In fact, mealtimes will become an Olympic sport."

"Three babies are a challenge," he agreed. "Did you ever think about having a multiple birth?"

"Yes, I did, but I really didn't believe it would happen." She rubbed her stomach.

"Are they jumping around?"

"Always. But that means they're healthy, right?"

"Yeah, or one of them is getting squeezed out by her sisters."

He pulled in at a barbecue place. "Barbecue doesn't bother you, does it?"

"No. I love it. Of course, I love Mexican food, too, but the girls don't." She chuckled.

"So we'll avoid Mexican for a few more weeks." He spoke without thinking, but the long silence that followed got his attention.

"What's wrong?"

Bri gave him a stubborn look. "You talk like we'll be eating together a lot. I appreciate your support, but you need to—to develop a social life. I can assure you the ladies of Austin will welcome you with open arms."

"You mean friendlier than the staff at the hospital? Wow, I'll be in hog heaven, as my dad says." He could've told her he didn't want any other Austin ladies. Just her. But not yet.

He parked the car and came around to help her down.

"I can manage," she protested, standoffish again.

"I thought maybe the girls were sleeping and you jumping down might upset them."

She glared at him.

After they were inside the restaurant and seated and the waitress had taken their order, he asked, "Who are you naming Eleanor after?"

She appeared surprised by his question. "Why do you think I'm naming her after anyone?"

"I don't know. I was worried that she'd be upset. Emily is named after your mother, and Elizabeth after mine. I didn't want Eleanor to feel slighted."

"Elizabeth is not named after your mother. You must stop saying things like that. It's causing talk all over the hospital!"

"Stay calm. And tell me about Eleanor."

Abruptly, she said, "She's named after my grandmother."

"Oh, good. Are you going to call her Ellie?"

"I don't know. I hate to make those decisions until after I meet her. All three girls will have different personalities."

"Yeah, it's amazing how quickly they develop an attitude, isn't it?" he said with a chuckle.

"Do you keep track of the babies you've delivered?" She needed to believe he was thinking of babies in general and not her babies specifically. It was too easy to start to lean on him, as she had done in New York.

"Actually, I want to invite the mothers and babies that we deliver back once a year for a get-together. I've been meaning to talk to you about it. With

McCallum Wing's reputation growing, some of them may be too far away, but I'd like to try.''

Bri liked that idea. After they'd received their food and started eating, she asked, ''Will you use it for scientific study, or just as a social gathering?''

''I'd like to do both. Have them fill out some forms from which we can produce solid data. And just get a chance to see the results of our hard work.''

''Maybe you'd better get the doctors started on making a list of questions they want to ask their patients so you can all contribute to the questionnaire.''

''Right. Especially since we're beginning to fill up.''

''Do we have more patients?''

''Three more patients. Madeline Sheppard had success with one of her fertility patients. Looks like it will be another set of quadruplets, but the mother is only a few months pregnant.''

''Who?'' Bri asked hurriedly.

Hunter stared at her. ''I don't remember. A common name, something like Green or Gray, definitely a color.''

She released her pent-up breath. ''Oh.''

''Ah, I'd forgotten your sister-in-law is undergoing treatment with Dr. Sheppard.''

''Yes. Sometimes I feel so guilty, having three babies when Maggie can't have even one.''

''It's not your fault, honey. You didn't do it on purpose.''

''No, but—never mind.''

He tried to think of another topic of conversation, but she reminded him he hadn't mentioned a third patient.

"Who's the third patient?"

"Another set of twins. Our first set went home today."

"Oh, good. They were doing well. The mother was very happy with our performance."

"Are you going to personally interview every mother before they go home?"

"I like to give their stay a personal touch. And I think I'll get more information that way than I will with a form."

"Probably true. You're very dedicated to your work, aren't you?"

"Isn't that a good thing?"

"Yeah, but I was thinking about your condemning tones when you said Jackson and Adam were workaholics. Sounds like you set yourself some pretty big challenges, too."

"You're thinking I'm going to neglect my children, aren't you? I'm not going to do that!" She glared at him again.

"Whoa! I didn't say that. I know you'll be a good mother. But you're going to wear yourself out. Maybe you can hire another assistant. Train her the way you want and do more supervising than actually performing the tasks yourself."

His idea didn't impress her. "Maybe you'll stick to your side of the business and leave mine alone.

Unless you feel I'm not doing my job. Then, of course, you can complain. As I will if I don't think you're doing your job.''

''Bri, you're getting upset over nothing.''

''Am I? I'm trying to support my family, and you keep suggesting I not work.''

''I'm not suggesting that, but I'm glad you don't have to. You'll be surprised how much energy three babies take.''

''And you know this because you've had triplets? You're like most male ob-gyns. You think you know everything, but you've never experienced any of it. I think that's why women ob-gyns are becoming more popular.''

''I'm sure. However, a number of them have never been pregnant, and even if they have, they've seldom had multiple births.''

''But at least they've experienced female problems!'' she said, putting down her fork and continuing to glare at him.

''Why are you picking a fight with me?'' he asked.

''I'm not. I'm simply disagreeing with you. And I'm ready to go home.''

Well, so much for the brief thaw in the cold war, Hunter thought. Bri seemed determined to fight with him. Maybe the gossip at the hospital had gotten to her. It was easier for him to ignore it because he didn't know those people who were talking. And the man was never condemned for having babies out of wedlock.

Should he offer marriage again?

No, she wouldn't listen to him. Okay, so he'd keep his distance and encourage Abby to keep close tabs on her patient.

But soon he was going to make his move.

Chapter Fourteen

"Hunter, please tell me you're not calling to find out
what Bri is having for lunch," Abby said in disgust.
The man had driven her crazy for the past two days,
wanting to know if she'd seen Bri, what she ate,
whether or not she was getting enough sleep.

"No, I'm not!" he assured her. "I wanted to see
if her checkup was at the same time as last week."

"I thought you were trying to avoid her?" He'd
explained to Abby that he was going to keep contact
with Bri to a minimum since he seemed to send her
blood pressure rocketing.

"It's my job to monitor the patients," he said
stiffly.

"You mean you're sitting in on every checkup?"
Abby knew better. She was even pretty sure she knew
why he was observing Bri so closely, which was why
she couldn't complain.

"Uh, no, but—but Bri—I mean, she's the first triplet patient."

She heard the edginess in his voice. "It's okay, Hunter. I understand."

Dead silence.

Finally, he said, "You understand what?"

"I understand that these are your babies."

More silence. "Why do you say that?"

"I say that because Bri wasn't dating anyone when she went to New York for a medical conference last spring. And I noticed on your bio that you were at the same conference. Even more, there's an awareness between the two of you that wouldn't be there if you were strangers."

"Is that part of the rumor mill?"

"No, not yet. Everyone's talking about a romance between the two of you. The theory is that you felt an attraction before. Now that you've found her again, you're still interested in spite of her condition."

When he didn't answer this time, she added briskly, "Her appointment is at ten o'clock, my first appointment so she can get out quicker. Same routine? You'll wait until we do the ultrasound before you come in?"

"Yeah, if you think she can handle it."

"Of course she can. I'll see you then."

Abby hung up the phone and leaned back in her chair. Amazing how things got screwed up in life. Two perfectly lovely people, blessed with triplets, couldn't seem to straighten things out. She was going to do what she could to help them, but some things were beyond her.

BRI WAS growing more and more tired, but she didn't want to tell anyone. When she undressed for her checkup today, she determinedly tried to look cheerful.

The nurse made no comment, silently assisting her onto the table and then leaving to find the doctor.

Bri had decided that her feelings were the reason for the tiredness. Since Saturday, she'd only seen Hunter from a distance. She'd apparently upset him so much that he'd dismissed any concern for her condition. He hadn't inquired about her health even once in the past few days.

She hadn't realized how much she would miss his concern and support. Her father had called to check on her. Her brothers had checked in. And Grace. But she missed Hunter's concern.

Abby came into the room. "Good morning, Bri. How's it going?"

"Just fine," Bri responded, a bright smile on her face.

"Sleeping well?"

She wasn't that good a liar. "Well, the girls move a lot at night."

"Any discomfort?"

Bri chuckled. "You mean other than the normal discomfort?"

Abby grinned at her. "Yeah. Anything abnormal?"

"No. I think we're all fine."

Abby directed her for the physical exam. Then she ordered her nurse to prepare Bri for the ultrasound.

"Hunter is coming in, as he did last week. That won't upset you, will it?" Abby asked.

Bri nibbled on her bottom lip before saying, "I know he has a job to do." That would be the only reason he would be here. It couldn't be because he had any interest in her, she was sure of that.

"Good girl." Abby nodded to her nurse who went over and opened the door.

Bri could feel his presence, but she tried to keep her eyes on the monitor.

Abby took up the ultrasound roller and rolled it over Bri's stomach, pressing into her skin. "There are our little ladies," she said, a smile on her lips.

"You're about thirty-one weeks, Bri. The girls are doing well. We're past any critical problems. You can deliver any time now without endangering the girls, so I want you to remember that. If labor starts, don't panic."

Bri stared at Abby. "You're telling me it won't be long now?" she asked, unable to stop her lips from trembling.

She almost jumped off the table when a big warm hand squeezed hers.

In a cheerful voice, Hunter said, "You can't stay pregnant forever, Bri, even if you love it."

She groaned, then tried to smile. "Thanks, I'll remember that."

"Remember this, too. Everything's going to be all right." Hunter's authoritative tones would've convinced anyone.

"Yes," Bri said softly. She wanted to believe him. But her mother had died delivering her children. While intellectually, Bri could explain why she shouldn't be worried, she was forced to admit that emotionally, she was.

"What he's trying to say," Abby added, smiling, "is that everything is fine. Any additional time in the womb can't hurt, but we're fine."

Abby looked at her nurse. "Peggy, help Bri dress, please."

Then she and Hunter left the room. Bri released a pent-up breath, staring at the door longingly.

Peggy patted her shoulder. "There now, everything's fine. You heard the doctor."

Bri hadn't even realized she had tears on her cheeks. She hurriedly wiped her face and smiled at Peggy. "Of course it is. It's just these stupid hormones. They're out of control."

BRIANA DIDN'T SEE either Abby or Hunter when she returned to her office. As soon as she got there, she picked up the phone and called Caleb on his cell phone. "Caleb? I need—I need to talk with you privately. Can you come to my office?"

He told her he'd be over at once.

Then she pulled out a clean piece of paper and hand-wrote a long paragraph. Then, covering the paragraph, she drew a signature line. Then she wrote a brief paragraph and another signature line.

"Lisa? Could you come in here?" she called.

"Sure," Lisa called and entered her office. "What do you need?"

"I'm going to sign this paper. I want you to witness my signature and sign to that effect."

"Of course. What is it?"

"It's—it's private. All you're verifying is my signature."

"Okay."

After Lisa left her office, Bri put her head down, squeezing her eyes shut, hoping to hold back the tears.

"Sis?" Caleb called as he rushed into her office. "Are you all right?"

She sat up and wiped her cheeks. "I'm fine. You got here quickly."

"I was in the building. Are you in labor?" Caleb asked, a slight panic in his voice.

'No, I'm not. I'm fine. But I want to give you something in case—in case something goes wrong."

"Don't talk that way. Nothing's going to go wrong."

She smiled. Maybe it wasn't her best smile, but she tried. "Of course not. But—but I've been lying about something and I don't want that on my conscience." She handed him the folded paper.

Slowly he read the paper and then looked at her. "What do you want me to do with this?"

"I want you to put it in a safe place and give it to Dad if—if something happens to me."

"Did something happen to make you worry?"

"It—it won't be long now."

"Bri—" he began. Then he stopped and began again. "Everything's going to be fine. I'm going to call you every night before you go to sleep. And you keep my number written out beside your bed. You call me at once. I'll get you to the hospital in no time."

"I know you will, Caleb. You and Adam and Dad, and Maggie, too, have been wonderful. It's meant a lot to me."

"That's what family is for," he said and leaned over to kiss her cheek. "You okay, now?"

"I'm fine. I feel better now that I've—taken care of that."

"Okay. How about lunch? Want me to buy you lunch?"

Bri smiled at her younger brother. He wasn't comfortable with the emotional stuff, but he wouldn't back away when she needed him. Love swelled in her heart. Her family was terrific!

"Thank you, but I think I'll have Lisa bring me some lunch here. I can work and maybe knock off early for a late-afternoon nap."

"Good idea. Okay, I'm off then. But you call me if you need anything."

HUNTER WONDERED if his policy of avoiding Bri was a good idea. She seemed a little shaky today. And he agreed with Abby. He didn't think it would be long now. He was surprised at the nervousness that filled him. After all his experience he was facing this delivery as a first-time father—a new experience—and no one would know.

He tried bringing his concentration back to his work, but Bri's face filled his mind. He saw the fear in her gaze, the panic that something might go wrong. It was important that she remain calm. Maybe he should stop by her office every once in a while so that—

"Dr. Callaghan, Caleb McCallum is here to see you."

"Send him in." He stood and moved forward to greet Bri's brother.

"What happened today?" Caleb's hazel eyes were filled with concern.

"What are you talking about?"

"Bri! What happened at her checkup?"

"Abby told her it wouldn't be long now. That's all."

"So everything's all right?" Caleb demanded, his voice intense.

"Yeah, everything's fine. Why?"

"She just called me, insisted I come at once. I thought she was in labor."

"No. What did she want?"

Caleb stood there, his hands on his hips. "I'm not supposed to show anyone unless something goes wrong. But you already know."

"What are you talking about, Caleb?"

"You can't tell her. Promise me."

"Okay, I won't tell her."

Caleb pulled a folded piece of paper out of his back pocket.

Hunter took it from his extended hand, suddenly nervous about what he was going to read. "Are you sure?"

Caleb nodded.

Slowly, Hunter unfolded the piece of paper and noted the two signatures first. Then he began reading. His head snapped up. "She's acknowledging me as the father!"

"Yeah. That's why I was afraid something had gone wrong."

"No, but she's worried."

"Why?" Caleb demanded.

Hunter didn't want to be brutally frank, but he had no choice. "The same reason you, your brother and your father are worried. Your mother died giving birth to triplets. Even though there's no reason to worry, and you understand that in your mind, your heart tells you to worry."

"Yeah." Caleb slumped down in a nearby chair. "Tell me again everything's all right."

"Everything's fine. Do you think I'm going to let anything happen to my girls...or my woman?"

"I hope not. We're counting on you, doc."

Hunter folded the paper Caleb had shown him. But he was reluctant to hand it back to Caleb. "Can I keep this?"

Caleb hesitated. "I promised Bri that I'd keep it safe until—until after the delivery."

"I swear I'll do that. But it means a lot to me that she made sure that I would be acknowledged as the girls' father. Did you know one of them will be named after my mother?"

Caleb appeared startled. "No. How did that happen?"

"Just a lucky coincidence." Hunter grinned at Caleb. "But I'd like to keep this."

"Okay." He cleared his throat. "I guess you deserve that."

"Thanks, Caleb. And I'll be keeping a closer eye on Bri."

"Good. Me, too."

Hunter sat back in his chair as Caleb left. Bless Bri for her honesty and honor. He'd instinctively recognized her goodness in New York. Now he had proof that she would do the right thing. And bless Caleb for showing him.

He reached for the phone. "Hi, Lisa. It's Dr. Callaghan. Does Bri have plans for lunch?"

After hanging up the phone, he strode into Helen's office. "I'm going to be having lunch with Bri in her office if you need me."

BY FRIDAY, Bri was feeling better in one sense. Hunter seemed to be keeping tabs on her again. More unobtrusively, but he was around.

But she was also feeling worse. The girls seemed

to be gaining weight rapidly. Or she was imagining that they were. It was getting more and more tiring to make it through each day.

She was really looking forward to getting home, eating a good meal and going straight to bed. Several of her friends had asked her to go out tonight, but she'd refused them all. It was just too much effort.

A rap on her door startled her, but she smiled when she saw Hunter. "Hi. What's up?"

After closing the door behind him, he strolled in and sat in front of her desk. "I wondered if you'd take pity on a bachelor and ask me to dinner at your place. I checked with Alice, and she said she'd fixed plenty."

Bri was surprised. While he'd checked on her often at work, he hadn't been back to her condo. "Of course. If Alice says there's enough, I'm sure there will be."

He studied her. "About ready to switch to half days?"

She wanted to protest, to assure him she could make it just fine. But she couldn't, and she wasn't going to risk her girls' health for her pride. "How did you know?"

"You've dragged a little lately. And I heard you turned down your friends for tonight."

"And they told you?" she asked, her voice full of surprise.

"Yeah. For some reason, they think I have some pull with you, Ms. McCallum." He shot her a teasing

look that raised her blood pressure. For all the right
reasons—feeling attractive because of the way a man
looked at her—except that she was as big as a house
with babies. No man would be interested in her now.

"Uh, well, I really am too tired for a night on the
town."

"Too bad. It's going to be a lousy baby shower
without you." He waited for her to realize what he
meant. Then he said, "Do you think you can make it
after a good dinner and half an hour's rest?"

"Of course. Oh, how awful of me. I didn't realize—they shouldn't have gone to so much trouble."
She thought about April and Annabelle's proddings.
Even Maggie had called and tried to get her to go
out. "Why didn't they tell me?"

"It's supposed to be a surprise."

"But you told me," she pointed out.

"Yeah, but I know how stubborn you are. Here's
how we're going to play it. Your father invited me
over for the evening and I talked you into going with
me because I don't know him so well."

"At my father's?"

"He offered April his house and his housekeeper
when Maggie told him about it. Even though it's
ladies only, he wanted to contribute to the shower."

"How sweet of him," Bri said, tears filling her
eyes.

"Your hormones really are working overtime,
aren't they?" Hunter asked, leaning forward. "Are
you really too tired to go?"

"No. I wouldn't miss this for the world. But where will you and Dad go if it's ladies only?"

"Your brothers are meeting us down at the Lone Star for a beer."

"Okay. Thank you for making sure I get there."

"No problem. Now, pack up and go home. Stretch out on the couch until I get there."

"Good idea. And I think I will work half days until the babies come, starting Monday. You were right about it getting to be too much."

He stood, leaned over the desk and kissed her, a brief but potent kiss. "Good girl." Then he walked out.

She stood there, breathing deeply, hoping to regain control of herself before she faced Lisa. The man certainly knew how to send her blood pressure soaring.

Bri organized her desk and retrieved her purse. Then she went out to Lisa's desk. "I know it's early, but I'm leaving. I'm going to have to go to my father's this evening to accompany Hunter, so I'm going to take a nap first."

"Dr. Callaghan's going to your father's?" Lisa asked, her eyes rounded in innocence.

"Yes," she said with a disgusted air, hoping to conceal her knowledge of the shower from Lisa. "Hunter said he didn't want to go by himself. He's only met my father once." She shrugged. "Part of the job, helping him settle in."

Then she hurried away.

Two hours later, while Bri still lay on the couch as

ordered, drifting in and out of a light doze, her door-bell rang. Alice hurried to let Hunter in.

He immediately came to the couch as Bri managed to sit upright. "How you doing?"

"Fine. I've been resting the entire time. I'm sure after I eat I'll feel even better."

"Good girl," he said again.

She was disappointed that there was no kiss this time. She was getting greedy.

Alice thought Bri knew nothing about the shower, either. Fortunately, Bri had thought of that before she gave the secret away. Dinner was ready early. It was delicious, as usual, but Bri didn't have much of an appetite.

Hunter urged her to eat a little more as he was packing away his dinner, hungry as a bear.

"You must've worked very hard today, Hunter," Alice said, a pleased smile on her face.

"I did, Alice. And I ran five miles in the Wellness Center this morning."

Bri groaned. "That makes me tired just to hear it."

"You'll be back in shape soon, honey. Don't worry."

"No. I'm not." What a lie, but everyone was so busy encouraging her, she had to make the effort.

"We've got a few minutes before we need to leave. Why don't you go lie down again while I help Alice with the dishes?"

"I'm okay. I don't need to—"

"As your doctor, I say you do need to rest," he said, smiling, but he also winked at her.

"Oh, okay," she agreed, though her initial response was to inform him that Abby was her doctor. But it was clear he needed to tell Alice something.

When they got in the car and left, she asked him what he'd told Alice.

"I left all my numbers with her. I told her it wouldn't be long before you delivered and to call me if she was worried about anything." Then he reached in his coat pocket. "I'm telling you the same thing." He pulled out a business card and handed it to Bri.

Great way to keep her calm for the shower, she decided.

Chapter Fifteen

"Be sure and act surprised," Hunter reminded her as he helped her down from his vehicle.

"My memory hasn't disappeared along with my figure. I remember."

"Yeah, but you're not very good at lies."

"I told you I'd practice."

She marched up the driveway of her father's large home, wondering how they thought they'd surprise her with fifteen cars parked in the driveway and along the street. Cars she mostly recognized. They must've invited half the hospital!

The housekeeper who'd replaced Grace, Milly, told her her father was waiting in the family room. Bri nodded calmly and led the way to the back of the house. When she opened the door to the large, comfy room, it was filled with women.

They all stood and yelled Surprise! and Bri gave them a shocked expression. "What are you doing here?" she shrieked. Then she turned to Hunter. "But you said my father—"

Jackson McCallum stood. He'd been sitting among the ladies. "Isn't this great, Bri? Your friends are throwing you a baby shower!" He seemed as excited as her friends.

"But I thought you'd invited Hunter over."

"I did. We're going to meet your brothers at the Lone Star. You ladies have fun." Jackson gave Bri a hug and then shoved Hunter out the door ahead of him.

Bri was left to face her friends. They were all there, including her assistant, Lisa, and Hunter's assistant, Helen. She noticed her sister-in-law Maggie sitting beside Dr. Madeline Sheppard, the fertility expert who was helping her and Adam. Bri wanted to make her way to Maggie's side and find out how things were going. To her surprise, she even saw Alice, sitting beside Grace. Maybe that was why Hunter had driven slowly.

April took her arm and led her to a large chair. "We saved this one for you since you're the guest of honor. We're only going to play two games, though, because we know you need your rest. Abby warned us," April tacked on, waving to Abby. "But we found a couple of real cute games we couldn't resist."

Bri grinned, but she hoped April would keep to her word. The effect of dinner and a nap was already wearing off. "I'm ready," she assured her friend.

The first game was a word puzzle. They had to make words from the letters of each of the three girls' names. The three prizes, plastic baby bottles, were, of course, passed to Bri. Then they had a game that asked crazy questions of the expectant mother. Each guest asked a question that had been passed out. It was fun for a while. Until they got to Annabelle.

She'd taken the paper passed to her, but the game had already started. She didn't read her question herself until it was her turn. "What did the father say when you told him he was going— Uh, this isn't a good question. Let someone else go next!" she suggested, her cheeks red.

April hurriedly agreed. But the next question was about the daddy, too.

April said, "You know what? I'm tired of games. Let's eat. That's the best part." She indicated the big coffee table filled with covered trays. "Maggie, can you uncover the trays on your side? Let me fill a plate for Bri, then we can all dig in."

Abby patted Bri's arm. "You stay put."

"I will. I think I'm going to start doing half days next week, Abby. I've been getting really tired."

"Good girl."

That was the same response she'd gotten from Hunter. Without the kiss. She had to stop thinking about him. He was being nice to her. But that didn't mean he was interested in a future with her.

She fingered the card in her pocket. She shouldn't call him when she started labor. She'd call Abby, the way she was supposed to. Abby could call Hunter if she wanted.

"Bri?" April said anxiously.

Bri looked up. "Yes, April?"

"Here's your food. I'm sorry I didn't check out that second game better."

"Don't be silly, April. I'm not upset."

"Are you feeling tired?"

"A little. But sugar will pep me up. I'll probably be dancing on the coffee table before the night's over," she assured her friend with a grin.

April smiled back and went to fill her own plate.

While they ate, the discussion turned to hospital matters, since most of them were connected with the hospital.

"How's Jenny doing?" Bri asked. "I didn't visit her today."

Several people shrugged. Then April said, "I stopped by her room today. I've been checking on her since she has no family. She couldn't get comfortable. Seemed a little down."

"Dr. Beaumont checked her today," Annabelle added. "He didn't say much about it, but he frowned a lot."

"Some doctors just frown," Madeline Sheppard said. Since she was a doctor herself, everyone laughed. "You can't tell by that. Maybe he had a hot date the night before and didn't get much sleep."

"Dr. Beaumont?" Annabelle said with a gasp. "Oh, I hope not. What will I dream about if he gets hooked?" she asked with a laugh.

"Well, there's always Dr. Callaghan. He's definitely dream material. I heard he spent a lot of time with Barbara in physical therapy the other day.''

''Really? The only person I've noticed him hanging around is Bri!'' Joanna, manager of the cafeteria, said.

''Anything going on?'' Annabelle asked, looking at Bri.

''All I can say is if he picks me over any of you slim, beautiful women, then he's either blind or you all have bad breath!'' Bri grinned to make sure they all knew she was teasing.

The chatter continued even as they started Bri opening the gifts. She was touched by all of them. Grace had handknitted three little sweaters in pink, yellow and green. Apparently her friends had discussed the colors, because she got baby blankets and even tiny sleepers in those three colors.

''You coordinated everything so well. I'll admit I haven't prepared as well as I should. I have three baby beds sitting in boxes at home. My brothers promised they'd put them together before I brought the babies home.''

''They'll keep their promise,'' Maggie assured her.

''I know.''

Bri did get a minute alone with Maggie toward the end of the party. ''Is everything going all right?''

''Yes. Dr. Sheppard is wonderful. She thinks we have a chance. And she made Adam feel good about the process. That was a big step.''

''I'd heard she was good. I'm glad it's true. I

should be taking notes so I can be prepared when it's your time for a shower.''

Maggie's eyes filled with tears and she squeezed Bri's hand. ''I hope I get a turn.''

''Me, too.''

''Bri, is Dr. Callaghan going to pick you up?'' one of the nurses asked.

''I don't know. Needless to say, we didn't discuss that since I thought we'd both be here. Anyone want to drive me home?''

There were several offers, and Bri considered that point settled. But the nurse, a blonde who Bri and her close friends considered to be a little full of herself, said, ''I'm hoping he comes back. He was hitting on me the other day, and I want to give him some, ah, encouragement. I wore this dress just for him.''

Since she was showing a lot of cleavage, and the skirt had a split up the side of her thigh, the other women had been sure she hadn't worn it for them.

The sound of footsteps and the opening of the front door told them the men had returned.

Bri smiled firmly. ''Maybe you can get Hunter to give you a ride home, Rita. Who knows what will happen in the dark.'' Then she resumed talking to Maggie. She wasn't going to get upset just because Hunter was flirting with nurses at the hospital.

''The nerve of her,'' Maggie muttered.

''Just be glad she's not after Adam,'' Bri said. ''At least she's focusing on an unmarried man.''

"Yes, but I thought—I mean Hunter has been—everyone says—"

Bri squeezed Maggie's hand. "He takes his job seriously. It's nothing personal."

Then she pushed herself up from the chair. "Hi, guys. Hunter, April has promised me a ride home, but Rita needs a lift if you don't mind."

He frowned at her. "There's no need to draft April. My car's big enough for two of you."

Rita laughed. "I don't know. Have you looked at the size of her lately?" She fluttered her eyelashes at Hunter.

Caleb stepped forward and Bri cringed, worried about what he would say in her defense. However, Hunter stopped him and assured Rita there was plenty of room. Then he organized her brothers to help him load the gifts.

Almost before she knew it, Bri had thanked everyone and been loaded into the front seat of Hunter's SUV. Rita was sulking in the back seat.

When Hunter got behind the wheel, he asked Rita for directions to her house. She lived quite a way from the hospital. Hunter looked at Bri. "I'd better take you home first, so you can get to bed, Bri. Is that all right with you, Rita?"

"Very all right," she purred.

Bri gritted her teeth and said nothing. She should get used to seeing Hunter with beautiful women. But she wished he had better taste than Rita.

When they reached her condo, after a silent ride, Hunter got out to walk Bri to her door.

"I can make it, Hunter. There's no need to keep Rita waiting."

"I told you my mother raised me to have good manners." He grinned.

His words reminded her of their time in the deli, and she couldn't help smiling back.

"There aren't any rats around here, are there?" he asked, teasing her.

"No, just bats."

"Why didn't you tell me? I have a phobia about bats."

"Yeah, right." They reached her door, and she had turned to thank him when his beeper went off. He checked the number, then asked to come in and use the phone.

As soon as he dialed the number, he only spoke once, saying he'd be at the hospital at once.

"What about Rita?" Bri asked, afraid he'd ask if Rita could stay with her.

"I'll take her with me and put her in a cab. But Jenny Barrows has gone into labor and Zach can't stop it. I want to be there to help him. It's going to be a tricky delivery."

"I'm coming with you."

"You're not coming with me. You need your rest!" he said emphatically.

"I can sleep all day if I want. Tomorrow is Saturday. I want to be there for the first quadruple birth. Either you give me a ride, or I call a taxi.''

''Bri—you can't—''

She pulled back on the jacket she'd just taken off and headed for the door.

''Dammit! This is crazy.''

She ignored him.

He followed her downstairs and helped her into the back seat. Rita had already moved to the front seat.

''What's going on? Has she gone into labor?'' Rita asked.

''No, but Jenny has,'' Hunter said as he got behind the wheel and started to the hospital.

''Jenny? Who's that?''

''The teenager having quadruplets,'' he explained briefly.

''You're her doctor?''

''No, Zach Beaumont is.''

Bri was glad she knew Hunter was a good driver, since Rita seemed intent on distracting him.

''I'm sure Dr. Beaumont can manage without your help, Hunter, darling. And I had special plans for when we reached my place.''

Bri figured the woman couldn't spell out her intentions any clearer than that. She held her breath, waiting to see if Hunter put her in her place.

''Sorry, Rita, I'll have to take a rain check. I promised Zach I'd be there.''

Well, not exactly a rejection. Bri wanted to slap

him. Okay, she'd told herself—and him—there'd be other women. But not in front of her!

No one said anything the rest of the drive. When Hunter parked his vehicle in the hospital parking lot, he dug out his wallet and gave Rita a couple of twenties. "Take a cab home. Sorry I couldn't take you."

"Me, too," she said in the purry voice again and leaned toward him, her lips puckered.

He pretended not to see them, getting out of the car and coming around to open Bri's door and lift her down from the seat. Then he rounded the SUV, with Bri at his side, and locked the doors as soon as Rita got out.

Without another word, he hurried into the hospital, holding Bri's hand.

He tried to argue Bri out of coming into delivery one more time. "Look Bri, her babies are early. I can't promise they'll all survive. I don't want you upset."

"I understand," she murmured, her gaze focused on the door behind him.

"You'll have to wear a mask and gown," he pointed out, as if that would discourage her.

"I know." Then she circled him and pushed through the doors.

One of the nurses helped her don the mask and gown and showed her where to stand to be out of the way. She wasn't surprised to discover Annabelle already in the room, talking softly to Jenny. And she felt sure April would be prepping the nursery and would be in shortly to help with the babies when they were born.

Just as Hunter strode in, scrubbed and ready to assist, April slid into the room. She saw Bri and came over at once.

"You're easy to recognize, even with a mask on," she whispered.

"It's my disguise as a blimp. Gives me away everytime."

"What did you do with Rita?"

Bri smiled under her mask. "Hunter gave her some money and told her to take a cab home."

Jenny screamed, grabbing their attention.

"I'd better get over there. Are you sure you want to be here?"

"I'm sure," Bri whispered.

She watched Hunter lean over and say something to one of the male nurses. He left the room, then came back in pushing a chair the height of a bar stool over to Bri.

"Dr. Callaghan thought you might get tired."

"Thank you," she murmured and managed to climb into the chair. She appreciated Hunter's thoughtfulness. Without the chair, she probably wouldn't have made it longer than half an hour.

Four hours later, all four of Jenny's babies had been delivered. Though she hadn't been in labor long, the births weren't easy. One baby had been touch and go for a few minutes, but the staff had performed a miracle and resuscitated it. Bri breathed a sigh of relief.

Jenny had lost a lot of blood, but they had her receiving a transfusion before she left the delivery room.

Bri asked one of the nurses about her condition, and the nurse assured her that Jenny would be all right.

Then Bri slipped away to the nursery where they'd taken the babies. She watched the four nurses, April being one of them, wash the babies and prepare them for their first night on earth. They were so tiny.

"I've been looking for you," Hunter whispered, startling her.

"Don't worry about me. I'll take a taxi home," she said, staring at the babies.

"Yours are already bigger. She was only twenty-seven weeks. You're thirty-one weeks, Bri. Your babies are going to be fine."

"Yes," she agreed quietly as exhaustion slammed into her now that the tension was over.

Hunter wrapped an arm around her and led her away.

She dozed off in the car. He awakened her and guided to her door. "Where are your keys?" he asked.

She dug into her jacket pocket and pulled them out. Hunter unlocked the door and led her straight to her bedroom.

"Do you need a drink or anything? Want some milk?" Hunter asked.

"That would be nice."

"Here's your nightgown," he said, and left the room. Only after he'd gone did Bri realize he'd opened her dresser drawers until he'd found where she kept her nightgowns. She had the nightgown over her head, pulling it down as he came through the door.

"Here's your milk."

"Thanks." She drank part of it and put it on the bedside table. "Later," she mumbled and slid into bed.

Hunter covered her up.

"Lock the door," she managed to say and that was the last she remembered.

WHEN SHE FINALLY awoke the next day, it was almost noon. She stretched and rubbed her stomach as the girls started making demands.

"Easy, there, girls. Mama had a rough night," she whispered.

She wasn't eager to leave her bed. She shouldn't have gone to the hospital last night, but she wanted to see the team in action. They were impressive. As soon as she found something to eat, she'd call the hospital and find out how Jenny and her babies were doing.

She stretched again, resting just another minute, promising the girls she'd eat so they could get some food. "How about scrambled eggs? Or I could add cheese and ham and have an omelet. Mmm, that sounds good."

But she still didn't get up. Her bed was too wonderful.

"Okay, okay, I'm moving," she promised as the girls jumped about even more. With a sigh, she said, "You three are so demanding."

She slid from the bed and made a trip to the bathroom, as she always did first thing in the morning. There wasn't much room for her bladder, and it frequently felt like the girls did a tap dance on it.

A couple of minutes later, she emerged from the bathroom to find Hunter standing at the door of her bedroom, a tray in his hands.

"What are you doing here?" she shrieked, startled by his appearance.

"Serving you breakfast. Hop back in bed."

The smells filling the air made her stomach growl. "How did you get in? Didn't you lock up last night?"

"Sure, but I pocketed your keys, since I figured you wouldn't need them."

"What if people think you spent the night? You're going to completely ruin my reputation!" she snapped.

"Are you going to eat this breakfast or not?"

She crawled back into the bed, glad she was wearing a long gown. "Hunter, I'm serious. You shouldn't have taken my keys and come over this morning. Someone might think you'd spent the night."

He set the breakfast tray beside her, since it wouldn't fit over her stomach. "Eat your breakfast."

"You made a ham and cheese omelet?" She couldn't believe he'd read her mind.

"I hope you like it. It's one of my favorites."

"Mine, too."

"Guess that's something else we have in common."

She'd almost forgiven his appearance when the doorbell rang.

"Who could that be?" Bri wondered, an uneasy feeling filling her.

"I'll get it."

"No, Hunter—

He ignored her protest.

Bri heard voices. Then footsteps. The bedroom door opened, and Rita was glaring at her.

"Well, I see you'll go to any lengths to snare a man, Ms. McCallum!"

Chapter Sixteen

Bri took a deep breath. "Are you here for any particular purpose, Rita?"

"Yes. I'm here to collect my man," the woman spat out.

"Collect away," Bri suggested, but she did glare at Hunter.

Rita turned her back on Bri. "Hunter, darling, I've been looking for you all morning. I want to make up for not, uh, entertaining you last night."

Bri pretended disinterest, but she watched Hunter closely.

"Rita, I think there may be some misunderstanding. I didn't intend anything to happen between you and me. You're an attractive woman, but I'm focusing on my career."

"Oh, I see. You think Jackson McCallum's bucks are more important than sex appeal. Well, I'm glad to know what kind of man you are."

She turned around and stomped back out of Bri's bedroom, followed by Hunter.

Bri lay there, steaming. Hunter was parading his women in front of her? And telling everyone he was after her father's money? She never wanted to see him again!

He walked back into her bedroom.

"Get out! And take all *your women* with you!"

Hunter studied her with no apparent alarm. "What are you talking about now?"

"You come parading your women in my house? And you don't understand what I'm talking about?"

"*My women* consist of you and three baby girls, and you know it. I haven't had so much as a date since I made love to you, much less sex. I was trying to let Rita down easy so she wouldn't spread rumors all over the hospital. She is most definitely not connected to me in any way."

"She said you hit on her. And she said you were hanging around Barbara in physical therapy. Not that I care what you do. I want nothing to do with you."

"Bri, you're being ridiculous."

"Just go away!" she said again, afraid she'd start crying in front of him if he didn't go away.

"Bri—"

"Go!"

"Fine, I'll go. But call me if you need me."

So he left. And Bri cried a long time, hating that he'd left. He'd probably followed Rita, who had a small waist and a flat stomach. Unlike Bri. That thought brought on more tears.

She fell asleep, worn out by her out-of-control emotions, crying over things that even she didn't believe. When she finally woke up later that afternoon, it was because of wonderful scents coming from the kitchen.

"Hello? Is someone here?" She pretended she wasn't hoping Hunter would answer.

"Just me, dear," Grace called. "Hunter called and said you were having a difficult day." She came into the bedroom, took one look at Bri and hurried to the bed. "Whatever's the matter? You look like you've been crying!"

"I have, but it's just silliness. Hormones. How sweet of you to come over."

"Have you been in bed all day?"

"Yes. Except now I need to excuse myself." Bri hurried to the bathroom, leaving Grace standing there. When she came out, Grace had straightened her bed and had the covers turned down invitingly.

"Slip back into bed, darling, and I'll bring your dinner to you."

"I think I'd better eat at the table, Grace, and stay up a couple of hours at least, or I'll turn into a slug."

"Whatever you think, dear Bri."

They ate together, and Grace maintained a conversation that demanded very little from Bri. Afterward, Bri sent Grace home with a hug and a warm thanks.

"You're sure you'll be all right?" Grace asked. "I'll be over tomorrow to cook for you again."

"No, Grace, I'll manage. Alice has frozen some things for me. You take care of Douglas. I know he likes to go fishing on Sunday afternoons."

"He doesn't need me to bait his hook," Grace assured Bri.

"Still, I know you enjoy going with him. I'll be fine." Bri was feeling terribly guilty about her childish tantrum. And that's all it was. She'd been tired and easily irritated. And she'd taken it all out on Hunter.

Once Grace was gone, Bri cut herself a piece of cobbler left over from the other night, put it in the microwave and loaded it with ice cream. She was indulging herself.

Should she call Hunter and apologize? No, she'd e-mail him on Monday. And keep her distance until after the babies came. Being near him unbalanced her and made her act like a love-starved animal in mating season.

She only had a few more weeks. She would be all right. She'd just go back to bed as soon as she finished her dessert. She'd read that book she'd intended to read when Hunter had given her a foot massage.

When she did go to bed, all she could think about was Hunter. And she fell asleep with no more of the book read than before.

BRI DID e-mail Hunter on Monday morning with an apology and a suggestion that they avoid each other until the babies were born. He didn't respond. However, he didn't show up at her office, either.

Since she was going home at noon, there wasn't a lot of time anyway. On Monday, she ate at Austin Eats before she went home, since Alice wouldn't be there until one. By that time, Bri was in bed, taking a nap.

She followed the same pattern on Tuesday. She was a little worried that she didn't seem to feel any more energetic than she had before, when she was working all day. She wanted to call Abby and ask her about it on Wednesday morning, but everyone was in turmoil about what had happened during the night.

"Did you hear?" Lisa asked her as soon as she got in. "That teenager, Jenny? She ran away!"

"What?" Bri asked in shock. "Where did she go?"

"No one knows. But she left a note for April."

"A note? What did it say?"

"She left the babies in April's care."

Bri needed to talk to her friend, and find out what the hospital was doing about the situation. "I'll be back in a few minutes," she told Lisa as she hurried to the nursery where April worked.

"April!" Bri called when she saw her friend in the nursery with the four tiny babies. "What happened?"

April handed her a piece of paper. "She left this

note in my sweater pocket. I'd laid my sweater on my chair when I went to prep a delivery.''

Dear April Sullivan,
I know you'll love my babies and take good care of them so I want you to have them.

Bri read the note several times. ''Oh, my. What's being done?''

''They called the police. They've questioned me, but I don't know anything.''

''How are the babies doing?''

''They're fine. Still weak and on oxygen, but doing better every day. But it will still be a while before they can leave the hospital.''

Bri saw the tears in April's eyes. She gave her friend a hug. ''Let me know if there's anything I can do to help. Do we need more nurses on duty?''

''No, there's plenty, unless you decide to have your three right away. Then we'll need more. But everyone's prepared for that possibility. We just weren't prepared for a runaway mom.''

Bri left April, knowing how upset her friend was. Everyone had talked about how attached April was becoming to the babies. Bri was afraid her friend was facing heartbreak.

Back in her office, she received a phone call from her father.

''What's going on over there? They're reporting on

the radio that the mother of the quadruplets ran away!''

''I'm afraid so, Dad. We've called the police.''

''Are they going to find her? I don't like this kind of publicity for the hospital.''

''It's not the hospital's fault, Dad. We've taken very good care of her. And the babies are improving every day. But she's a teenager. It's pretty easy for an adult to be overwhelmed by having more than one baby. A teenager with no money and no family might decide she couldn't handle it.''

''Humph! I think I'll tell Caleb to investigate. He's still the best cop in town!''

''Dad, he's not a cop any longer. Are you sure—''

''A son should be willing to do his old man a favor. I'm calling him.''

Her father hung up the phone, and Bri replaced the receiver. But her concern was for Caleb. He avoided emotional situations. Would he want to investigate the disappearance of Jenny? She hoped her father didn't badger him into it.

''Abby called to remind you of your appointment,'' Lisa said from the door. ''It's in ten minutes.''

''Oh, right. Okay. I'll see you in a little while,'' Bri said as she left her office.

Soon she was on the examining table. But when it came time to do the ultrasound, there was no Hunter.

''Is Dr. Callaghan not coming?'' she asked quietly.

''He's trying to handle the disappearance of that

young woman, Jenny. I guess he doesn't have time today," Abby said with a smile.

But Bri knew the truth. She'd disgusted him with her outburst, her childish temper. She bit her lip to hold back the tears and watched as her babies came into view.

"Just four weeks until your due date," Abby pointed out. "You've done very well, Bri. And I really expect them to be born at any time. How are you feeling?"

"Still tired, even taking half days."

"I'm not surprised. They've grown this past week. You're carrying around more baby. Rest as much as you can, and call me as soon as you feel anything different."

"I will, of course. Do you think they'll find Jenny?"

"I don't know."

"Dad thinks it's bad publicity."

"It is, even though I don't think the hospital is the reason she left. But some people will think so."

One of the girls gave Bri a solid kick. "Ooh! That hurt."

"Where?" Abby asked at once.

"One of them is under my rib. It's nothing out of the ordinary."

Somehow, without Hunter present, the checkup wasn't much fun. And Bri, too, felt the babies were coming soon, which made her nervous. What she wouldn't give for a foot massage now. Or just Hunter smiling at her.

"It's your own fault!" She reminded herself in the elevator. Fortunately she was in it alone.

When she got back to the office, she checked with Lisa to see if there was any change in the situation, but there didn't appear to be any. Then she checked her messages and her desk. Nothing was urgent, what little there was.

Suddenly, Bri decided to go on home. She didn't want to be at work. Telling Lisa she had something she needed to do and that she wouldn't be back today, she slipped out of the hospital.

She crossed to Austin Eats to pick up lunch and take it back to her place. The café was alive with questions about what had happened at the hospital. Bri remained silent, got her food and hurried out.

She ate lunch and slid into bed afterward. She was getting to be very good about taking naps. Today, however, she couldn't seem to get comfortable. She ended up on the sofa, watching soap operas and reruns, twisting and turning, trying to find a position that would let her relax.

Alice came in and cleaned, stopping to have conversation with Bri, which made her feel better. She didn't want to be alone today.

She guessed it was because she had hardly worked at all that she didn't have much appetite at dinnertime. Alice urged her to eat until Bri almost burst into tears.

After Alice left, Bri was so uneasy she began to pace the living room.

Finally she sat down on the sofa to watch more TV. When she got up to go to the kitchen, her gaze fell back on the sofa.

And she panicked.

HUNTER was tired.

It had been a long day, handling the police and the press, plus trying to be sure everything that should be done was.

Yet, with all of that, it was Bri who was on his mind. He'd had to miss her examination. He'd called Abby when he got a minute. She'd said everything was okay, but she'd sounded worried. He'd pressed her, but she'd said she couldn't put her finger on what was bothering her, but she'd stop by the office to see Bri in the morning.

He couldn't do anything else tonight. Bri didn't want him dropping by. That much she'd made clear. He sat on the bed in his hotel room and ate his take-out food, staring at the television, even though he couldn't have said what was on it.

When the phone rang, he almost didn't answer it. It was after nine o'clock. He'd told the press everything he knew. But it could be the police, saying they'd found Jenny. So he leaned over and picked up the receiver. "Hello?"

"Hunter, I'm bleeding!"

The panicked voice was Bri's. She was bleeding, like her mother. "I'll be right there!"

He grabbed his keys and raced to his car. As soon as he got on the road, he pulled out his cell phone and hit the quick-dial button that would ring the hospital. He explained that he was bringing Bri in. They should call Abby and prepare for their arrival.

When he reached Bri's place, he sprinted up the stairs and rang the doorbell. She opened the door at once. Her eyes were wide with fear, and tears had left tracks down her cheeks.

"It's okay, Bri. I'll take care of you," he said and swept her into his arms.

"My bag," she said, her voice weak.

"We'll get it later."

When he reached the SUV, she handed him a folded towel. "So I won't mess up your seat," she said, almost sobbing.

He did as she asked, putting the towel down before he set her upon it. Then he strapped her in and ran for the other side. He was trying to be calm before her, but he was finding himself playing the role of an expectant father, not an experienced doctor.

He drove as fast as he could, and they were at the hospital three minutes later. He stopped in front and two nurses rolled a gurney out the door. By the time he got around the vehicle, they were ready for him to put Bri on it.

"Hunter," she called, sounding even more panicky as the nurses began pushing her toward the door.

"I'm right here, honey. Everything's going to be fine. They've called Abby for us." He looked at one of the nurses for confirmation of that statement.

"She's scrubbing up, doctor."

"See, she's already here, honey. Everything's going to be fine."

It didn't take long to reach the delivery room. Abby had a calm smile on her face as she gave orders to the nurses for Bri's care.

Hunter drew several deep breaths before he conferred with Abby in a low voice, so Bri wouldn't hear. He and Abby worked well as a team as they staunched the bleeding and set up a transfusion. Bri began having contractions fast and furiously, as if Mother Nature knew it was time for the babies to be born now!

Abby and Hunter decided to let nature take its course, with a little help from them. Not half an hour after he'd gotten Bri to the delivery room, Emily made her appearance. Eleanor was next and she came fairly quickly after Emily, just three minutes apart. But Elizabeth wasn't in a hurry. It was almost ten minutes later before she was born.

Three beautiful baby girls.

"Bri, they're all perfect," Hunter told her. "Emily is already sleeping, Eleanor is complaining, and Eliz-

abeth is simply staring at everything with big eyes.''
He bent down and kissed Bri. ''They're beautiful.''

''Did—did you get the bleeding to stop?''

''Yeah, it's stopped. You're going to be fine.
We've improved a lot since your mother gave birth
to you and your brothers.''

''Did you call Dad?''

''I'll do so as soon as they take you to recovery.
There'll be a nurse there with you. I don't want to
leave you alone.'' In fact, Hunter didn't want to leave
her at all. He clasped her hand tightly, so relieved
that his girls had made their appearance. And he and
Abby had been able to make sure Bri was okay.

They wheeled Bri into recovery. A nurse was waiting for them.

''Keep an eye on her, and watch for signs of bleeding. If there's anything wrong at all, get a doctor,''
Hunter instructed.

''I've been a recovery nurse for thirty years, doctor.
I think I can handle everything.''

''Be sure, nurse, because this is the mother of my
babies. I don't want to take any chances.''

The woman gasped, but Hunter didn't care. Bri had
called him when she was worried about the babies.
And he intended to marry her as soon as possible.

He stepped into the hall and dialed Jackson's number. ''Jackson? It's Hunter. Bri just delivered the
girls. Everyone's fine.''

"She's fine? She didn't die?" Jackson demanded, urgency in his voice.

"Nope. She's fine. Can you call Caleb and Adam? I want to get back to Bri."

"She's fine?" Jackson asked again.

"She's fine. The girls are fine. We're all fine. By the way, the babies are mine. I'll explain when I see you."

"O-o-okay," Jackson said slowly, as if he wasn't sure what he'd just heard.

Hunter hung up and reentered the recovery room, just as Abby came from the delivery room.

"Abby, are you going to check her again, be sure there isn't any additional bleeding?"

"Of course. But you can do it if you want."

"No. I'm discovering why they don't encourage doctors to work on relatives."

"She isn't one of the girls, Hunter. You're not kin to her."

"Not yet. But I'll be her husband as soon as it's possible," he assured Abby, beaming at her.

"Well, I'm relieved. Does Bri know that yet?"

"No. I was afraid to discuss it before the babies were born, because she kept getting upset."

"I wish you all the best. Did you call her father?"

"Yes, I did."

Abby checked Bri and assured Hunter she was doing fine. "I'm going to go look at the girls and make sure the nurses called a pediatrician."

"Good. Tell them hello from their dad."

"Will do," Abby said, grinning widely. The nurse was staring at Dr. Hunter Callaghan. Abby knew the news would be all over the hospital by morning.

Bri slowly woke up, knowing something was different. When she finally opened her eyes, she realized she was in the hospital. Her girls had made their arrival. She tried to sit up, and Hunter opened his eyes.

He was sitting in a chair beside her bed. He stood and leaned over her, gently kissing her lips.

"Are the girls all right?" she asked hurriedly.

"The girls are perfect. We were waiting for you to wake up before I took you to your room. Want to drive by the nursery and see them?"

"Oh, yes, please. Hunter, thanks for coming for me so quickly. I'm afraid I was panicking a little."

"That's understandable. I'm glad you called me."

She blushed, knowing she'd promised herself she'd call Abby. But Abby wasn't who she'd wanted when she realized she might die. She'd wanted Hunter. She'd wanted to feel his touch, to see his smile, to feel his protection. As she always would.

He released the lock on her bed and pushed her into the hallway, turning a sharp right to go down the long corridor to the baby nursery.

"How big were they?"

"They were all over four pounds. Emily was the biggest. I think she weighed 4 lbs, 12 oz. Eleanor was the feistiest one with the strongest lungs. But she only weighed 4 lbs. 3 oz. Then Elizabeth, who wasn't in a hurry, weighed 4 lbs. 8 oz.''

They reached the windows that allowed the family to keep an eye on the newest arrivals. Hunter stopped the bed and helped Bri sit up a little so she could see the babies.

Tears filled her eyes.

Her father spun around. ''Bri! There you are. Those little girls are so beautiful! How do you feel?''

''Fine, Dad. I'm fine.''

Caleb and Adam and Maggie hurried up for a big family reunion. There were a lot of compliments for the three baby girls.

''So I understand there's going to be a wedding,'' Jackson finally said, looking first at Bri and then Hunter.

Bri stared at her father, then snapped her gaze to Hunter. ''What did you say?''

Jackson pointed to Hunter. ''While you were still in recovery, he said you two were getting married. He said he's the daddy.''

Hunter grinned and kissed Bri on her lips. ''Don't even think of denying it, honey. I've been telling everyone they're mine.''

Bri remained silent so long Hunter got worried. Finally, she said, ''I'm not denying you're the father, Hunter. But that doesn't mean you have to marry me. I won't ask that of you.''

Hunter cupped her cheek. "Honey, do you know why I took this job?"

"Because it's a good one."

"Nope. I took it so I could see you again. So I could find out if you were no good...or if you were my dream lover, as I'd thought until I found you gone."

"You really did come to look for me?" Her voice wobbled, but she kept her gaze fastened on Hunter.

"I really did. I wanted us to find a way to be together, because I knew what we'd found was special."

"But you didn't know where I was!" she exclaimed.

"Yes, I did. Once I learned your last name, I knew where to find you. I just wasn't sure I wanted to find you. But when I got a chance, I jumped at it. Then you walked in the door, pregnant. It took me a day or two to work everything out. But you already had me under your spell again."

"Oh, Hunter, I—I was so hurt."

"I don't understand any of this," Jackson protested. "Are you getting married or not?"

"Please, Bri?"

"Are you sure you love me?"

"With all my heart. But you'll have to share me with the girls. My four ladies." He kissed her again.

"Well?" Jackson insisted.

"Oh, yes, Dad, we're getting married," Bri said,

her gaze still fixed on Hunter. "Oh, I've missed you so much," she said, her arms going around his neck.

There was a cheer around them, and Hunter looked up, startled to discover about fifteen members of the staff listening to his proposal.

But he didn't care. He'd found his true love once more. He had no complaints.

"Will you move in with us? I don't want to live in a hotel," Bri said.

"I didn't get a chance to tell you. I got the house. By the time the girls can go home, we'll be moved in."

"Oh, Hunter, that's wonderful!"

He thought so, too, and swept her back into an embrace that he'd developed a need for in New York City, locked in a deli eight months ago.

Epilogue

Briana awoke the next morning when April shook her awake. "Hey, lazybones, breakfast will be here in a few minutes."

"Lazybones? I gave birth to three babies. I think I should get to sleep for days!" Bri exclaimed, but her smile told April she didn't mean it.

"True, but I've heard you're having company for breakfast. I thought you might want to comb your hair or something."

"Visitors this early?"

April grinned. "Well, when you're the doctor in charge of obstetrics—"

Bri was filled with excitement—and happiness. She hadn't admitted it to herself, but she'd feared Hunter might've changed his mind. "I need a shower!"

"I'm not sure—"

"Please, April," she pleaded.

"All right. A quick one. Stay in bed until I get everything ready."

Ten minutes later, Bri was back in bed, her hair

still wet, but the rest of her ready for a special visitor. The door opened, after a brief knock, and a nurse came in carrying her breakfast tray, followed by Hunter, carrying a second tray.

"Do you mind having company for breakfast?" he asked with a smile.

"I'd love it," Bri assured him.

April followed the other nurse out the door. "Ring us when you want the trays collected."

Hunter didn't move until the door had closed. Then he set the tray on a nearby table and reached for Bri, his arms sliding around her. "How are you?"

With his arms around her, she felt better than she'd ever felt. "Wonderful." Then he kissed her and she felt even better.

"You haven't changed your mind?" she asked afterward, her voice a little wobbly.

"I'll never change my mind. And I'll never leave you or our girls. We're going to be married as soon as you feel up to it."

"Today?" she suggested.

"I think you'd better recover for a couple of days at least." He kissed her again.

"Will it always be this wonderful?" she asked as she relaxed in his arms.

"Yeah. The seven months we were apart, I missed you every day. I was mad at you, but I still wanted to be with you."

A knock on the door brought a frown to Hunter's

face. "Come in," he called. The frown went away when he realized who had arrived.

A deliveryman came in carrying two large vases of roses, one with white roses that had deep pink streaks in them, the other with pale yellow roses with pink streaks. He announced, "Flowers for Miss Emily Callaghan and Miss Eleanor Callaghan."

Bri stared at the flowers while Hunter showed him where to place the vases.

"I'll be right back," the man said. When he entered again, he carried another vase like the others, this one filled with peach roses with pale yellow streaks for Elizabeth Callaghan. But in his other hand he had a vase with two dozen scarlet roses for Briana.

When he'd gone, Briana asked Hunter to bring her the cards. Each of the cards for the girls said, "Welcome to our family, love Daddy." Her card said, "Thank God I found you again. All my love, Hunter."

Tears filled her eyes and she slid her arms around his neck for another magical kiss. "You're wonderful."

"There's just one thing we need to negotiate," he murmured, and Briana's heart clutched.

"What?"

"In a year or two, we might do this again, and have boys this time so I won't be outvoted all the time."

"How about I just promise to vote with you?"

"I don't know. I'm thinking one of these girls will have to be a really good shortstop, then."

"We'll see."

Another knock on the door interrupted them. Hunter frowned again. "I thought they were going to leave us alone!"

But these guests were welcome. Two nurses brought in three little girls, identically perfect. The first nurse announced, "Here are your babies, Mommy and—" She stopped abruptly, staring at Hunter.

He stood and crossed to take one of the girls. "And Daddy," he said with pride.

"And Daddy," the nurse repeated.

Briana reached out for one of the babies and Hunter took the third baby, too.

Bri smiled at Hunter, his arms full of babies, and her own precious bundle, and believed in the future. Together, with Hunter, they were going to have a wonderful life, starting right now.

* * * * *

Don't miss
QUADRUPLETS ON THE DOORSTEP
by Tina Leonard,
next month's installment of
MAITLAND MATERNITY:
TRIPLETS, QUADS & QUINTS
coming to you from
Harlequin American Romance
in January 2002.

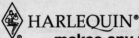

CALL THE ONES YOU LOVE OVER THE HOLIDAYS!

Save $25 off future book purchases when you buy any four Harlequin® or Silhouette® books in October, November and December 2001,

PLUS

receive a phone card good for 15 minutes of long-distance calls to anyone you want in North America!

WHAT AN INCREDIBLE DEAL!

Just fill out this form and attach 4 proofs of purchase (cash register receipts) from October, November and December 2001 books, and Harlequin Books will send you a coupon booklet worth a total savings of $25 off future purchases of Harlequin® and Silhouette® books, AND a 15-minute phone card to call the ones you love, anywhere in North America.

Please send this form, along with your cash register receipts as proofs of purchase, to:
In the USA: Harlequin Books, P.O. Box 9057, Buffalo, NY 14269-9057
In Canada: Harlequin Books, P.O. Box 622, Fort Erie, Ontario L2A 5X3
Cash register receipts must be dated no later than December 31, 2001.
Limit of 1 coupon booklet and phone card per household.
Please allow 4-6 weeks for delivery.

I accept your offer! Enclosed are 4 proofs of purchase. Please send me my coupon booklet and a 15-minute phone card:

Name: _____

Address: _____ City: _____

State/Prov.: _____ Zip/Postal Code: _____

Account Number (if available): _____

---

097 KJB DAGL
PHQ4013